CW01650644

THE GREAT TURNABOUT

THE GREAT TURNABOUT

being the Saga of a
young officer during
the final throes of the
Second World War

by

DAVID ENGLAND

Published by Ian Harrap at
THE PALLANT PRESS
13 The Pallant
Havant, Hampshire

CONTENTS

All the characters in this story are all imaginary. None is real and therefore concerns no person in particular.

ISBN 0 950 71414 3

Printed by Strand Press, Petersfield

CHAPTER ONE

Forward Looking

The sky hung grey-black over the Northumbrian countryside and the great house lay back, its silhouette flanked by comforting, if sombre, fir trees. I had heard much about The Hall which, before the Second World War, had housed a well-known, if eccentric, family of politicians and writers with friends on both sides of the English Channel.

Canadian troops had previously occupied the house, and it was rumoured that they had ripped up floorboards for firewood in the cold of a northern winter. Now the unit I was to join was billeted there.

What bad luck, I thought, to join your first unit as a commissioned officer three days before Christmas, especially with rumours of the 'second front' featuring strongly on the horizon for the next year. Where would we land up next Christmas? Perhaps in Heaven or Hell? Anyway there would be no leave this time round, for second-lieutenants were fair game during high days and holidays, and a duty officer would have to be found for every minute of the national holiday break.

Officer training had been arduous but exciting during the past ten months, and I had not had any leave, since the War Office needed to train as many officers as possible for the reserve units which would stand in readiness to back up the first waves of troops landing on the beaches across the English Channel.

Never mind - que sera sera! I must brace myself to accept the battle conditions I should find once I reported to the Adjutant who surely lived just inside the great door of The Hall.

I approached and expected to be challenged by a sentry. A smart salute should get me off to a good start I thought. I reached the door but no challenge; I knocked but no answer; I pushed the door and it opened; I walked into the vestibule - no lights and no-one in sight! Had I come to the wrong location? Improbable, since I had passed my tests in map reading with flying colours and my rail warrant had indicated that I should alight at the local station.

The time was 15.30 and there was still just enough natural light to admire the grand staircase and the doors to the left and right of the hallway.

Nothing for it but to knock at one of the doors - where was the orderly room?

This was the Field Headquarters of a Divisional Signals unit and it was possible that the unit was deployed around the house and heavily camouflaged. Then I saw the door marked 'Adjutant' and hesitated no longer. A light tap, but no answer; a good rap with the knuckles and the door gave under my hand. There I was in what should have been the Presence, but his chair was empty and the room deserted.

It was now getting quite dark, it was cold and cheerless and I thought of Scrooge and poor Bob Cratchet.

There was a sudden crash somewhere above me, a rending of wood and a loud curse. A leg appeared through the ceiling and then disappeared again. I dashed out of the room, headed for the staircase and ran up to the first landing.

There was Henry, my fellow second-lieutenant as I was to learn later.

"Who the Hell are you" he said, and "Get me out of this mess!"

I went to his help and tried to straighten his leg.

"For Christ's sake leave my leg alone" he said, obviously in much pain, "I think it's broken".

"We must get help for you, but where is everyone?" I said.

"They are all out on a bloody exercise" he growled "and won't be back until 18.00 hours. I was left in charge of the house and vehicle park out at the back. I came in for my hurricane lamp but forgot that the ruddy Canadians had reduced the upper floors to bare joists before they pulled out. There's a field telephone in the Adjutant's office, so be a good chap and 'phone through to the mobile switchboard and ask for an ambulance - I would rather spend Christmas in hospital than in this God-forsaken dump - some smashing talent among the nurses in the local military hospital" he said.

Before I did what he asked, I returned to the staircase and introduced myself - "I'm David England and I've just passed out from the O.C.T.U."

"You'll pass out here once the Adjutant gets hold of you!" he said "and you won't have me to share the duties with you over Christmas."

What an anti-climax at the start of an army career, I thought, as I made my way round to the back of the house to find the signalmen who were dug in around the mobile rear-link Signal Office.

"Do you have your papers, Sir?" said Corporal Higgs. "The Adjutant has given me strict instructions to allow no access to the Signal Office for unauthorised persons while this exercise is in progress."

"Oh! Here are my papers and you see I have been posted to this unit, Corporal, but now we have an emergency on our hands so don't waste time. Lieutenant White has fallen down in the house and broken his leg. Please ring for an ambulance." "Christ, Sir," he said "Lieutenant White is the only officer left at Rear Headquarters."

"Well, you've got me now so I'll take over until the unit returns."

The ambulance arrived within an hour but before we got Henry off the premises I asked him where I should go until the unit returned.

"Whatever you do don't go up them stairs" he said. "You'd better go back to the Signal Office and await the return of the hordes. Of course you will be billeted upstairs eventually but you'll need a guide if you are to avoid my fate."

CHAPTER TWO

Out with the Unit

"You've come up from Catterick, have you? The Lord help us" exclaimed the Adjutant when I finally got my interview the next morning.

"As if I didn't have enough to do trying to work my present shower into a unit fit for Monty's drive on to the Continent!"

A bland man of about 26, he was smartly dressed and liked to wear his Sam Browne belt. He had dark hair slickly parted down the middle and I noticed nicotine stains on his fingers from heavy smoking.

"We were over strength when we came up here a month ago and now they send you, too! Since I suppose you're all theory and no practice, you had better spend the morning sharpening my pencils and do look at Unit orders. We've had one hell of an exercise with the Royal Artillery complaining about our inability to translate their gunner jargon - I think I'll put you out with the gunners next time. That'll blood you alright!"

"Thank you, Sir" I said.

"This afternoon you can join Staff Sergeant Willis who will be doing vehicle inspections in place of that clot White who put his foot through the ceiling while we were away. Oh, yes, and you will also become our Messing Officer in the absence of White. His catering was appalling and don't forget that I like plenty of marmalade with my breakfast."

"But Sir, I know nothing about catering. They only gave instructions in Mess-tin cooking in my old unit while I was in the ranks."

"Too bad, son. You'll just have to look up the manual and get on with it, won't you?"

"By the way, you'll have to watch out for friend Willis. He simply loves to wrong-foot young officers who hardly know a carburettor from a sparking-plug!"

How right he was, for when Sergeant Willis asked me to inspect and test-drive the big six-wheel heavy recovery truck, I started the great diesel engine all right and put the vehicle into first gear, but when I let in the clutch I stalled the brute! Of course all the other ranks were watching and the guffaws could be heard in the Great House itself!

Out on the Northumbrian moors with the gunners was quite a rude awakening. No doubt a delightful grouse moor on the 12th, but we were now into Winter and the peaty soil was holding the rains of Autumn. Our vehicles got bogged down and we had to organise squads of soldiers to place wooden planks or anything else we could find under the driving wheels before we could move around.

While the Royal Corps of Signals provided a link from Brigade H.Q. to the Field Artillery Regiment attached to our Division, the gunners had their own regimental signallers who had been trained to transmit precise directions for the 25-pounder guns and were quite unaware of the general Divisional procedures used by us. Thus, in no time at all, I found myself in the middle of an altercation between our two Sergeants who obviously disapproved of one another.

"Get your bleeding wireless trucks out of my lines" said the Gunner Sergeant "You're supposed to be in support, not in line with our guns."

"Well, if you had given a precise map reference with your target co-ordinates and, incidentally, your bloody regimental wireless frequencies, perhaps all of our vehicles would have been sighted correctly in the first place," shouted our Signals Sergeant with some feeling!

Such exchanges were frequent during the early days of

Such exchanges were frequent during the early days of 1944 while the division was shaking down for the big push into Europe.

I had a miserable Christmas on duty, at the beck and call of all the other officers and I was very relieved when my fellow lieutenant, Henry White, returned a few weeks later from his spell in the local hospital, to share the chores.

Henry, just short of 6ft. in height with a sallow complexion and a small well-groomed moustache, was full of the fun and games to be had with the nurses at the hospital and suggested that we both went to the next dance in the Town Hall Assembly Rooms. As well as the nurses there were a lot of girls whose boy friends had sadly been killed in Italy a few months before, while serving with the local regiment.

The next Saturday we managed to escape from our unit and, duly paunced up, we proceeded to the Assembly Rooms where Henry had arranged to meet his favourite nurse, Angela, who was bringing a friend for me. I'm not one for the blind dates but needs must when the devil drives, so I swallowed twice and went through the doors with some trepidation.

I need not have worried, for the girl who was waiting with Angela didn't look like the fast piece I had been led to expect. She stood with her shoulders slumped and head lowered so that I could hardly see her face. She was wearing a faded green velvet dress but her thin legs were clothed in a new pair of nylons. My heart went out to her straight way and I no longer felt embarrassed.

"This is Marjorie," said Angela. "She lives in town and lost her fiancé a few months ago. I had quite a job to persuade her to come tonight. She has just started as a Nursing Auxiliary with us."

"Hello," said Marjorie, "I'm not much of a dancer."

"Nor am I, but let's have a go" I said.

Northumbrian dancing is not dissimilar to Scottish and is accompanied by a squeeze-box and violin. Everyone was excited and enjoying themselves when the lights failed. Amongst a clamour of voices we heard a man call out that we should stand still until the fault could be rectified. There had been no air raid alarm, so we all did what we were asked to do.

Marjorie clung tightly to me and I put my arm around her. She had a lovely soft body and I don't mind telling you I was much put out when the lights came on again! We looked around for Henry and Angela but they had disappeared.

"Do you think they have gone for a drink?" Marjorie said.

"Could be", I said - but I thought quite differently. No doubt he had taken her off to some quiet spot for a snog or more! "Anyhow, don't let's worry about them - are you having a good time!"

"Yes" she said "but I feel quite guilty about it."

"I do know how you feel but you have got to go on living for the future, not the past. With any luck we should win in Europe with Monty's push and skill. He's not lost a battle yet, thank God."

Marjorie buried her head in her hands and began to sob.

"Don't carry on like that, Sweetie," I said, holding her close. "Won't do any good."

"It's all right for you - you haven't got to stay in this damned town and wait to hear of more boys being killed - might be you next time," Marjorie declared.

"Would you mind then?"

"Of course I would," she said with feeling.

"Anyhow, don't let's get morbid, for war is far away

tonight - come and have a drink, it will cheer you up."

As it happened, the evening was only just hotting up for Henry and Angy while I was consoling Marjorie. He had whisked his ladylove away to a discreet little pub in a side street not far from her hospital. Angy had matched him gin for gin during the dance and was, by this time, exceedingly flushed and animated.

"Let's have another one for the road," he said, pushing a double into her hand while fondling her rounded figure playfully. Angela threw her head back, closed her eyes and pressed her body against him.

"Let's get out of here" he murmured.

"Where shall we go?" Angy moaned. "Can't go back to the nurses' home with all that mob coming in and out of my room! Wait a bit though -" she took his hand from where it shouldn't have been and staggered out of the pub with a far from reluctant soldier in tow.

"Oh, bugger" he said as he stumbled over a kerb-stone and fell flat on his face. This woke Angela out of her reverie and the nurse in her took over.

"Come on, give me you arm and see if you can get up."

Remembering that Henry had only just recovered from a fractured leg, she really was concerned for him. He got to his feet all right but was limping badly.

"I had better take you up to the Casualty Ward" she said "just to make sure that you haven't broken anything again." In their drunken state, they took quite a few minutes to get to the Casualty Department which seemed to be in darkness except for one light shining through the glass doors.

"Let's leave it, love" said Henry. "I'll be O.K."

"No, I can't let you go back to camp like this, darling, and anyhow I don't want you to leave me at all - at least we must go inside to look at your leg."

They groped into the building and made for the dimly-lit room.

"Don't lets go in there, Sweetheart" he said, suddenly grabbing her and whisking her into one of the unlighted cubicles off the corridor.

"Oh, God, not here of all places" she gasped as she fought for breath. Henry wouldn't take no for an answer and started to undo her dress with sweaty and fumbling hands.

"No, don't do that! I know the boy in charge of the Casualty Department tonight and he will soon hear us and get suspicious."

"Blast him" said the lieutenant getting more persistent every minute. He had quite forgotten the pain in his leg and was now trying to unhook Angy's bra. She slapped him off and in doing so flicked the light switch, thus illuminating their arbour of love. Unfortunately for them, they had chosen an outside cubicle and before they knew it, faces were peering through the unblacked-out window from the outside and there was much ribald mirth and shouts of "Put that light out" from fellow nurses and doctors returning from the dance.

The noise, of course, attracted the attention of the doctor-in-charge of Casualty who swept the cubicle curtain aside to reveal our lovers clasped together in a heap on the floor! So much for illicit love-making after dances and the subsequent reprimands from an irate matron and a very tetchy Adjutant, in the morning.

Meanwhile, I had seen Marjorie home and had made another date with her. She suited me down to the ground and we simply liked to meet for a late cooked tea, then go to the cinema or sometimes a dance. She didn't smoke, and drank only when she was thirsty. Since I had to pile away far too much of the hard stuff during Mess Nights, I enjoyed a gentle half pint of shandy with this sweet girl.

In March, the Division was moved to the South and laagered up in the Salisbury Plain area, while our particular unit proceeded to the Isle of Wight in order that we could provide communications between the local observation posts around the Island and back to H.Q. on the mainland. I was put in charge of 'C' cable section with responsibility for maintaining all the line communications around the army units, Home Guard and Observer posts.

High Command were taking no chances with German paratroopers who, they thought, might try to land and prevent the safe build-up of invasion craft in the Solent area. They had learnt this sort of lesson in Singapore where the Japs had been able to turn the allied guns and use them to prevent the withdrawal, by land and sea, of our garrison who were in the event, stranded almost to a man.

Although the terrain of the Island was very interesting and varied, life was pretty dull after our divisional manoeuvres in the North, but Spring had its own attractions even if we did get the occasional air raid and German paratroop landing scares.

My trouble was lack of transport but I did manage to cadge a lift in an amphibian DWK on one occasion to visit Marjorie, on leave and staying friends on the mainland.

The distance from Cowes to Lee-on-Solent was only about eight nautical miles, but we had to pilot our way through numerous craft which were darting hither and thither between the dark green lines of moored invasion barges of all sizes and shapes. Landing Ships Tank, assault craft, Landing Ships Infantry, rocket firing ships - you name them, they were there. We quite expected to be challenged by one of the fast patrol boats policing these closely guarded waters and we had our answers ready if challenged, but nothing happened except that we felt queasy once or twice. Put that down to apprehension, since we were not officially allowed to leave the Island unless on official business, during those days of invasion build-up.

I had sorely missed the warmth of Marjorie since coming South and it was with excitement and anticipation that I travelled to our rendez-vous in the city of Winchester which was still open to free passage by civilians.

A friendly brother officer in Lee-on-Solent, where we came ashore, arranged a lift for me and, for the first time, I saw the vast build up of tanks and other vehicles waiting to board the vessels we had seen while crossing the Solent.

I knew that we had very little time together, so I arranged that we should meet at an Hotel where the food was still good.

My heart missed a beat when I saw how much better Marjorie looked. Her eyes sparkled and she was wearing a new dress and coat to match them.

"Do you like my new get-up, David? Thought it was time to snap out of feeling sorry for myself and get on with life."

"Good girl" I said rather fatuously. I took her arm and led her to the Restaurant, for we were both ravenous - in more ways than one, after some good wine.

"I can only stay for a few hours and I don't know when I shall be able to see you again. It is almost impossible to get on and off the Island now and I am not likely to be so lucky in finding unofficial transport a second time" I added.

"Oh" she said, looking sad and crestfallen. "I had hoped we could spend a bit of time together during my week's leave."

"I'm sorry, Sweetie, but there's simply nothing I can do about it."

She saw how unhappy I was, too, and began to cry.

"Tell you what - let's go to the cinema, then at least we

can hold hands."

"Do we have to?" she whispered; "It's so sordid in the back row!"

"There's not much alternative in this city" I apologised.

Our eyes met and before I knew it, I had taken her hand and led her to the Hotel Reception, where I found myself asking for a room. To my surprise, no questions were asked and we clung to one another in a most passionate way until it was time for me to return to my lonely Island aboard that army "Duck".

CHAPTER THREE

The First About Turn

There is always a calm before a storm and I soon got my marching orders to return to the mainland and to H.Q. situated on Salisbury Plain.

It was not long before the Colonel sent for me and told me that I had been transferred to the Wireless Communications Section.

"You will be issued with three high-powered field wireless transmitters and I want you to stow these out of sight, on your 3 ton trucks which have been allocated from the M.T. pool. You will then wait for your movement order, map co-ordinates and transmission instructions including frequencies - that's all."

I saluted and retreated from the Presence.

We were having some beautiful weather in May 1944 and I wondered whether the Colonel knew when the balloon was going up or whether this was just another false alarm. I was a little mystified by the Colonel's request to take trucks from the vehicle pool. Didn't sound like a push across the Channel to me; no waterproofing, no war stores and only personal arms to be taken.

My wireless operators reported for duty and we got our equipment together, including poles, pegs and guide ropes for outdoor aerial arrays, if required.

Abruptly, I was summoned to the Adjutant's office and he gave me a large package marked *most secret*, and my movement order with map references.

"Off you go, young England, and don't make a muck of this assignment," he muttered.

"Can I make contact with H.Q. while I'm away on detachment?"

"Not bloody likely, you damned fool" he said. "If we move our H.Q. I will get a message to you by despatch rider, otherwise return here at the allotted time - now hop it!"

I was amazed to discover that I was to travel *North* and not South or West. When we had reached rural Oxfordshire we laagered up in a field on high ground and made our first transmission - all in code, of course. The operators were very curious about our task and the Corporal in charge had queried our route more than once. "Begging your pardon, Sir, but are you sure of your map co-ordinates?" he said

"Quite sure, Corporal, and I am just as puzzled as you are, especially as we are to move even further to the North tomorrow." Actually we moved North-West and as we did so, column after column of vehicles passed us going in the opposite direction. Some of the columns were American, and the Yanks had a few words to say about our little convoy.

"Say, boys, are you heading for the Second Front in Iceland or summat?"

As we couldn't answer them we just kept our heads down and drove on.

At long last we reached the border country between Wales and England, and having made our last transmission for the day, a lone Despatch Rider appeared out of the gloom with a signal ordering our return to base.

"What a bloody waste of time" the Corporal was heard to say to his men.

I must have been very dim in those days, for not until after the war did I learn that our little squad had been part of a grand wireless deception plan to keep the Germans guessing while the invasion preparations were being completed.

Back at H.Q. things really were on the move and I was

told to dismantle the wireless equipment and prepare the trucks for a journey to the Base Ordnance Depot in order to load some of the unit's equipment for delivery to a supply ship berthed in London Docks.

"This is it" I thought, "Now the balloon *is* going up." I managed to navigate round London quite well and we had a Corps of Military Police dispatch rider to guide us into the Docks. We were naturally held up at the gates and my men and I had to prove our *bona fides* before we were allowed to proceed to the quay.

"No good coming in 'ere, mate" said the Dock gatehand "the boys are on strike!"

"On strike at a time like this?" I said.

"Yes, the boys say that they want extra cash to load this heavy duty material."

"Well. I have my orders to load this equipment and I have ruddy well got to do so."

"Can't do nuffin about that, Guv" he said.

I must say that I felt a bit panicky and I swallowed quite a few times. Still, must show some initiative, I thought, and by this time my men were watching me also, to see what I would do. I called my corporal over and told him to take over while I went to find a telephone in order to ring the Adjutant. This *would* happen when we are not carrying a wireless transmitter, I muttered to myself.

Finding a 'phone box was no trouble, but to contact the unit on an open line might break security, so I prepared my own little speech before dialling the call.

"Hello, Sir, this is England 'phoning from London."

"What the Hell are you doing there at this time of day - you are not on leave you know!"

"No, Sir, but I do have a bit of a problem. I arrived at my destination to find that there was a strike in progress. What happens next? Shall I come back?"

"Not on your life, Sonny. Here's what you do - parade

your men in full battle order and, you personally, give them bayonet drill on the dock in front of the dockies - see what that will do."

"O.K., Sir, I'll try it."

"Report back if you have no luck" he said and rang off.

"Thanks for the idea, Sir," I said to the Adjutant when we returned to the unit very much later. "It worked like a charm. The dockies took one look at that cold steel and I think for the first time realised that the Second Front might be for real and that they should put personal grievances behind them at such a critical time."

"Well done, David" he said with a warmth to which I was not generally accustomed, and dismissed me.

Since our stores were now loaded, I realised that time was short, and my heart leapt a beat or two when I was told to report to the Colonel's office the next morning. It was June 5th, 1944 and I was not the only one to be standing before the great man. We were told to stand at ease and we all held our breath. Then the bombshell fell:

"I have to tell you, gentlemen" he said "that you will *not* be proceeding across the Channel as had been envisaged but instead you are to report to the London District Assembly Centre to be kitted out for service in the tropics. I am afraid I cannot tell you any more than that - we shall be sorry to miss you in the unit during the next few weeks, I can tell you, but presumably higher command does know best. I often wonder about that, however, and just as we have shaken down into such a good unit, too. Never mind, good luck to you all - you may dismiss."

Lieutenant Henry White and I reeled out of that room in a daze and it took us some time to adjust to this very sudden and unwelcome news.

Next morning, we reported in at the Assembly Centre only to hear that the invasion of Europe had begun!

CHAPTER FOUR

Night Alarm

Speculation as to where we were to be sent was much influenced by the B.B.C. news reports which were issued almost hourly on D-day and the tense days which followed it.

Had our comrades of a few days before landed at the right beach-heads and all in one piece? I thought about my stores and wondered whether the freighter, which we had loaded so dramatically, had proceeded to its allotted assembly point prior to crossing the Channel. We soon heard that our boys had crossed the rough English Channel almost unopposed and that we had air superiority over the whole area. We also heard that the Airborne Division with whom we had shared the Salisbury Plain area, had landed both men and gliders on target, though not without many casualties.

Our reveries were soon shattered by the sound of the air raid sirens for this was London and many flying bombs were still getting through our defence network. These little-ram-jet pilotless planes were too fast for any of our fighters other than the Spitfires, Tempests and the new Gloster Meteor twin engined jet fighters. We had heard the daring of pilots of these machines who had risked being blown up in mid-air by approaching the V-1's, wing tip to wing tip, so that they could 'nudge' the little hornet-sounding ram-jets and turn them from their course, perhaps to fall harmlessly when their engines cut out over farmland rather than on the big cities.

The citizens of England had already learned to keep their heads down once the engine had cut. Those of us who were waiting for our movement orders at L.D.A.C. that momentous week were lucky, however, and we heard no ominous sounds in the sky above London before we were summoned to meet in the assembly hall of what had been the Marylebone Station hotel. "Right, Gentlemen," shouted the Commandant, "fall in and be counted. I am going to number you off from the right and all those with odd numbers are posted to East Africa, and all those with even numbers will go to West Africa." You could have heard a pin drop! We were all amazed - AFRICA - why should we go there in 1944 just as the long-awaited Second Front had started in Europe?

The Commandant had anticipated our incredulity and began to explain why this extraordinary action had to be taken.

"No doubt you are surprised to be told of such an unexpected destination at a time like this, but you will also know that the 14th Army in Burma is desperately short of personnel and General Bill Slim has persuaded the War Cabinet to provide him with two more African Divisions, one from the East African Rifles and another from the Royal West African Frontier Force. Each of these territories has already provided one division which is on active service.

"You young officers will be expected to train the new African soldiers from scratch and make them into a fighting unit within 3-5 months - you will then travel to India to receive final battle training at Divisional level. Now do you understand your assignment?"

We did, in no uncertain terms and having received the most hair-raising advice from a Staff Sergeant who had just returned from the Burma front, we proceeded to the medical room for our 'jabs' and issue of tropical kit.

"You can now proceed on leave but you will be on 12-hour recall so register your leave address with the Staff Sergeant on the desk." With this warning, we were dismissed by the Commandant. Much as I wanted to go to my home in Surrey to visit my anxious parents, I was longing to see Marjorie again, but how? She was on duty 300 miles to the North and once home I couldn't leave my family for a twelve-hour stretch without some awkward questions being asked like 'Are you serious about this girl?' I honestly didn't know the answer to such a question.

The war in the Far East sounded horrific and there looked to be no end to it. Frankly, I didn't rate my chances of returning to the U. K. very high, but I couldn't tell my parents that!

I resolved to go home first then 'phone Marjorie in the evening from a call box. My parents were super people and I didn't like this deceit but a telegram or letter telling her that I was going overseas was not permitted in war-time.

Our home was in the path of the Nazi flying bombs directed at London and so one member of the family was called upon to listen for engine cuts in case it was necessary to retire to the air-raid shelter which my father had constructed out of his old study.

After dinner all was quiet so I made my excuses and went for a walk. It was a lovely evening and almost mid-Summer. The birds were singing and the pigeons cooing. Couples were walking arm-in-arm in the lane just as if it were peacetime. In my situation, I felt quite divorced from sane ordinary life and almost ran to the call box so that I could hear Marjorie's reassuring voice - but no reply from her number. Oh God! what a let-down, I cried in frustration. I flung out of the telephone box, kicking metaphorical stones and walked at a rate of knots up on to the hill which looked out onto farmland and woods. A feeling of great isolation and loneliness descended on me. I went home and tried to be cheerful but my parents knew that something was wrong. They suggested that we went round to see some mutual friends, and after a few drinks very cordially offered, I felt a bit better.

I got up early the next morning and to my delight I managed to catch Marjorie before she went off to work. She was surprised to hear my voice and became very anxious when she heard that I was at home on leave.

"I know you mustn't tell me where you are going, but can we meet just once again before you go, my love. I can't bear to think that you, too, are now going off to war, perhaps never to return."

"Hush, sweetie - it's not as bad as that. We haven't been called yet and I may have quite a few more days' leave. Could you get off in time for us to meet somewhere in the Midlands?"

"Well, I can try, but we are very busy at the hospital and I am not sure that Matron will let me off," she said.

"Oh, surely she will when she knows why."

"But she doesn't know about us, and Ted - my ex-fiancée - lived almost opposite her house!"

"Well, can you 'phone me tonight at this call box?" I said.

"Why at the 'phone box?" she said, "- Haven't you mentioned me to your parents?" she almost sobbed.

"No, I - I haven't told them anything about us - you know what parents are like - they will expect us to become engaged and I just can't think of a permanent arrangement at a time like this."

"Why not?" Marjorie almost shouted, "Other people get engaged in similar circumstances,"

"I think it would be better if we didn't try to meet then, but you write to me just as soon as you can. *I* might not be waiting for you here if you do come back. *I'm* not engaged any more." She was crying and after a moment she rang off.

I was desolated but knew there was nothing I could do to resolve this problem.

As it happened, I had only two more days leave before we were recalled to L.D.A.C. so I had no more time to think about a future for Marjorie and me.

We all reported for duty once again and the following morning we entrained for our journey to an 'unidentified' port which we soon realised was Liverpool. As the train pulled into the docks station, I looked anxiously for the ship and saw, to my horror, a smallish coaster berthed at the quay at which we had stopped. I am a bad sailor and had expected at least a 5,000 ton United Africa Company steamer for the voyage out into the hostile Atlantic!

"Oh, God", I said to Henry White, who had also drawn an even number, "Here we go for a bumpy ride."

"Good Lord, son" he said in a rather patronising voice. "The boys on the Overlord run caught an unusual channel storm but we *are* now into flaming June - keep your pecker up!"

We gathered up our kit and walked towards the quayside only to be told to move on to the next berth at which lay a magnificent liner which we subsequently learnt belonged to the Royal Mail line. She had been on the South American run, up to the outbreak of hostilities and had been cruising during the summer months.

We were given four-berth cabins and our first meal was the best we had experienced since 1939. The stewards were Indian and we were given some magnificent curries during the voyage which brought us to Freetown, Sierra Leone after ten days of zig-zagging out into the Atlantic and then back again. We were escorted by two Destroyers until we were clear of the Straits of Gibraltar, then we were on our own, being a fast ship.

The ship, in fact, was bound for Cape Town and so we formed only part of its complement of passengers. Naval personnel, including WRNS, were in the majority but there were also some service families travelling out to join their husbands manning the Simonstown Naval base.

Henry White got very excited at the prospect of dating one of the WRNS and finally succeeded in attracting the attention of a rather mousy brunette in glasses. She looked so green that I determined to chat her up and warn her of Henry's excellent technique with the ladies. The ship was dry but we could buy soft drinks at the bar. After a couple of days my chance came and I managed to stand next to her while she was ordering a drink.

"I think you know my friend Henry White," I stammered.

"Oh yes, but I know a lot of officers - who are you?"

"David England is the name and we are bound for the West African station. Are you going on to South Africa?"

"Yes, but we have plenty of time before then," she said, giving me the sexiest come-on look I'd ever experienced during my short forces career. I retreated in some confusion and realised that what appeared to be sugar and spice wasn't always so nice! Henry was welcome to her charms but I felt that he would have to pull out all the stops to make first base with this most experienced chick!

As we neared the coast of Africa we smelt the stench of the rotting vegetation and centuries of open-ditch sanitation in the towns. The approach to Freetown is dramatic. The natural anchorage is surrounded by sharp-topped hills capped by palm trees and other vegetation. The town in those days nestled under these hills and many of the buildings were of wood with corrugated iron roofs. The African houses and stores were often thatched, however.

Most disappointingly we were not allowed to go ashore

and those of us who were to travel on to Nigeria were transferred in lighters to an old coasting tramp steamer much like the one we saw at Liverpool. We waved good-bye to our beautiful liner whose next stop was to be Cape Town and life for us changed abruptly.

We were shown to one of the holds of the tramp steamer by a steward who informed us that we would have to sleep in hammocks for the four-day voyage along the West African coast. The hold was very hot and the only ventilation appeared to be a circular canvas 'funnel' which emerged on the deck. On inspection, we found cockroaches climbing along the partitions and along the bulkheads. "I'm not standing for this" said Henry White and stormed out to find the ship's captain. The humidity was building up now we were stationary in the harbour, which is not far above the Equator. Just standing and waiting for the outcome of Henry's enquiries made me sweat profusely and I wondered how we would all fare when we actually landed in Africa!

The Captain was nowhere to be found but the Mate suggested that the officers should bring their bedrolls on to the deck when the boat had quietened down for the night. We all felt better when the old tub got under weigh and started her journey along the 1500 miles of tropical sandy-beached coast. We ate our food in the old teak-lined passengers' dining room and tried to imagine the scene during the 1920's and 30's when colonial government servants and United Africa Company employees dressed for dinner and listened to the gramophone over their coffee and liqueurs as the moon shone on the placid almost translucent tropical sea which was a home for gigantic turtles. Some people played bridge and others poker but never until they had checked out on the card-sharps and professional gamblers. The whisky and Van der Hum bottles would be on the tables and the bar steward would be run off his feet with the constant demands for top-ups.

Now it was wartime and the ageing ship was dry and we had to observe the blackout since enemy submarines were never far away. We did have a gramophone aboard, however, and we used to creep up onto the boat deck and organise our bed rolls around the air vents before setting the needle into the groove of an old 78 record.

It was fortunate that we only had four nights to endure because we had just six records to choose from. My favourite was 'Holiday for Strings' played by the inevitable David Rose orchestra. We were never far from the coast and the smell of Africa always prevailed! The turtles floated lazily just beyond the wash of the ship as she ploughed along at about 10 knots. Our first call was at Accra, then the first port of the Gold Coast. We anchored off the wide golden beach and watched the big surf canoes coming out to take off cargo and some of our troops. It had not been possible to build a mole of any sort because of the very exposed beach, and the strong undertow, and we were told that a commercial harbour had been built at Takoradi, some miles to the west particularly for the export of Bauxite.

While most of the freight-carrying canoes were by this time motorised, we still saw the glistening bodies of the athletic Africans paddling the older craft out to the ship in order to offer us fruit, leatherware and trinkets much as their counterparts at Port Said, Hong Kong and other famous ports, are accustomed to do.

There was much bargaining and we all ate well that night as we left port bound for our destination, Lagos in Nigeria. By this time we were so far away from the war that we forgot to black out our portholes after dark - and so when the alarm bells sounded loud over the quiet waters, we jumped like startled rabbits.

"Put those lights out, you damned fools" shouted an officer from the bridge - and we did post haste!

Accra was not all that far from the border with the then French Dependancy of Dahomey, a small state wedged between the Gold Coast (Ghana) and Nigeria, and it was a moot point in those days as to whether the allegiance of the people was to General de Gaulle or the Vichy Government.

Thus, we realised that a German submarine could be lurking off this coast, and our fears were substantiated when a dark object suddenly materialised on our seaward side.

The Dahomey coast was only a few miles distant and the Captain must have taken an instant decision for he turned sharp to port and made for the shore.

A conning tower loud hailer warned us in a gutteral voice to stand-to or be fired on, but we didn't stop.

"All hands and all army personnel to clear the decks" came the command and we all moved like lightning. Our ship was unarmed so there was no question of positive action on our part.

"Crikey - what a way to end the war" said one of our number. "If the Captain doesn't stop we shall be blown out of the water - and the Germans are not likely to pick us up!"

By this time a vague outline of the coast was visible and it was obvious to us that at the best, the Captain could beach the ship in neutral waters. The first salvo of shells from the submarine shattered the silence of the night as spumes of water cascaded on to the deck.

"Nearly got us, by God" someone said. The next salvo sailed through the derricks on the fo'c'sle and shattered the winch cables with a loud twang.

We thought that the third salvo had got us, but the great crunch, followed by a shudder, told us that we must have hit a mudbank. The ship came to a dead stop and she was a sitting target. There was dead silence once again, however, and we all scattered to our lifeboat stations and stood awaiting our fate.

After about ten minutes, someone from the bridge informed us that the submarine appeared to have vanished into the darkness just as quickly as it had come, but that we should continue to man our lifeboat stations with our personal arms and kit and await further orders. It looked as if one of our patrol boats had appeared on the horizon.

By this time it was after midnight and pitch dark. As the dawn came we were able to assess the situation for ourselves. We were, in fact, wedged tight on a sandbank and the actual shoreline seemed to be about a half mile away. The Captain had been reading his charts and it appeared that we were near to the port of Cotonou, not far from the Nigerian border.

In Lagos, our final destination, about 50 miles to the east, there would be tugs available to tow us off the sandbank. Should we break radio silence and request help, or should we send a boat ashore to assess our reception in French territory? This would be a risk for we might all be interned.

The Captain decided to radio for help pending a possible visit from the French authorities who, of course by this time, had us in full view. We were sitting off the old slave coast and some wit pointed out that centuries later it might be *our* turn to be enslaved in darkest Africa - what a turn-up for the book!

Fortunately, for us, a message was soon received from Lagos that a tug would be despatched to tow us into Appapa Wharf so all we had to do was to keep the French talking until the tug's arrival.

The tug and the French arrived almost together and after several hours of negotiation, the tug was permitted to tow us off into deeper water and away to Lagos.

The moments of tension gone, we looked ahead to the prospect of making our true landfall and we were not disappointed as we approached Lagos Lagoon past Lighthouse Beach and the long mole which led via the stinking mango swamps to Appapa Wharf where we eventually tied up.

CHAPTER FIVE

Strange Destination

Our introduction to Lagos Lagoon was encouraging for, to the left and right of the harbour mole lay the glittering silver white sands of Lighthouse and Victoria Beaches. The stench from dark green mangos was overpowering, however, as we steamed through the Lagoon to tie up at long last at Appapa Wharf built by the United Africa Company. To our surprise, it was a modern complex with control buildings roughly in the centre of a long quay with tall cranes. We were told that the terminal building actually had a flush loo, and that we had better make the most of it since we would not be staying long in Lagos en route for the jungle battle camp in the bush! What a queue there was that morning, and the humidity was so great that we were all sweating by the time we climbed aboard the trucks, to be taken around the harbour, over the iron Carter bridge onto Lagos Island and through the seething native town with its open drains, to the transit camp which turned out to be located in a pleasant coconut grove inhabited by vivid orange and black green iguanas, practising their press-ups on every occasion!

On the way we passed the white-railed Race Course and the European Quarter of Ikoyi which housed Government offices and the headquarters of industry, threaded through the busy streets and squares with their colourful covered markets selling everything from yams and cassavas, the local vegetable diet, to sewing machines and bicycles. Fruit at the camp was plentiful and we were to enjoy the coconuts, grapefruit, oranges and lemons, not forgetting the bananas, just ripe for the picking.

At this time, British West Africa was in a period of

transition between the old colonial rule, modelled on the Indian Civil Service practice and a more open system of government anticipating some form of independence after the eventual end of the War. We were to hear of a mystical figure called Zeke whose followers were pressing for immediate freedom for Nigerians. We soon realised that there were three distinct tribal groups concerned, but most of the soldiers we were to command came from the Northern plains and scrubland, far from the dreaded tsetse fly which had almost obliterated all meat-yielding mammals in the great Gombe forest and jungles of the South.

Having been given dire warnings about the tsetse, mosquitoes and creepy crawlies in general, we were sent to a place called Ilokomiji, some sixty miles north of Lagos and located in the heart of a great teak forest, where the only mitigating factors were the hordes of beautifully marked and coloured butterflies which ascended in clouds as we surprised them on the jungle paths and clearings.

Fortunately, we had arrived in the dry season so it was fairly easy to clear ground to erect our bivouacs around camp headquarters, which consisted of a field kitchen and latrines.

We were met by a fiendish-looking sergeant who had just returned from the Arakan Front in Burma and he immediately put the fear of God into us by telling us that we were to be sent, on our first night in a tropical jungle, on a compass march through the snake-infested bush, and - "Be careful, you lucky lads, for the green and black mambas frequent your bog huts as well as the jungle around here. They likes the warmth". One can die from a mamba bite in a few minutes unless an antidote is applied immediately.

We were here to train for the jungle-clad hills of the Arakan where the leeches have to be burnt off your legs and arms if you are foolish enough to expose them. Although the Gombe Forest was not so badly infested with these creatures, the mosquitoes could give you malaria and so we very quickly covered ourselves after dark that night. We had been given our mepachrine pills to help matters, but we knew that we must not march through the swamps in case the weevil-like creatures, which carried the disease Bilharzia, bored through the skin of our feet to put us out of action. This had happened to an earlier battalion whom we were now to replace in the Far East. "Look sharp, gentlemen", shouted the sergeant - "Let's be having you for your night march".

Lt. White and I looked at one another as we checked our compasses, and I swear that he had as many of those butterflies in his stomach as I did! We could have wished that those beautiful creatures could be let out to guide us away from the mambas and other creepy crawlies lying in wait for us.

Our small band of very white-skinned British officers left the jungle clearing for the unknown thickets of creeping vines, bamboo and dense vegetation which even in the dry season completely covered the ground between the tall trees interspersed with Jacaranda, brushwood and giant ferns. Cries of animals and birds could be heard above the beating of our hearts. We had to force a way ahead using machete knives and rifle butts to clear a path. We each took turns to lead with a No.2 giving directions left or right according to the compass bearing given to us by the sergeant. Suddenly a shriek of anguish came from our leader and we pressed forward to discover what was wrong. All at once, the air around us was alive with small objects and we felt sharp pain on our necks and faces. We were being attacked by a swarm of hornets whose nest had been bisected by the leader's machete. There was utter confusion while we each jerked and dodged to swat these beastly little creatures. Ultimately, order was restored, we circumnavigated the offending nest area and completed our mission, accompanied by the raucous laughter of the Burma sergeant who had known from the start just where the hornets' nests were located on our given compass bearing.

After our month of jungle marches and battle training in the bush we were told that we should be posted to a North West Frontier Force training battalion for duties with African troops who had just joined the Army. Talk about the blind leading the blind!

The white officers were told that they would form the nucleus of a new battalion to be part of the relief brigade destined to push further over the rugged and jungle-covered hills of the Arakan running down the coast of Burma. The 81st West African Division was to be withdrawn from the Arakan Front after stout service and our lot would take over their duties. We were told that there would be much 'carrying for head' in the infantry platoons as we would have to use tracks rather than the one road which was constantly under observation by the Japs.

The Indian Army generally provided mule trains for the heavy equipment, but mortars with their heavy bases, anti-tank rifles, Bren guns and their ammunition, mortar shells and grenades would have to be man-handled to allow for maximum mobility.

All this information but we had yet to start our soldiers' basic training!

Henry White and I had been posted to a battalion occupying a vast clearing in the Gombe Forest just under two miles from a large African town teeming with busy laughing Nigerians who came in from their jungle villages to buy and sell in the "mammy" markets which abound in all native towns in this part of the world.

There was very little hygiene, so we were relieved to learn that our meat came direct from the army depot at Lagos. All the meat on the native stalls had to be brought down from the North of Nigeria on the one single line railway which branched in the pleasant town of Kaduna to continue South to Lagos in the Western province and to Port Harcourt in the Eastern province. There were many stations on the way including the one in our town.

The great river Niger virtually divides Nigeria into its three zones of influence with the Muslim Hausa people to the North of the river, most of the Christians in the Eastern province (now Biafra) where the Ibo people live and the Yoruba people, many of them also Christians, living in the Western province. Most of our soldiers, however, were Hausa men from the North and amongst those already mentioned were many from the old French West African territories.

I was introduced to my men by an 'English teacher' who was very intelligent and wise. He spoke English in a slow and dignified manner and I suspected him of being a headman in his village although he never admitted it. He had come from a village to the north of Kano, the walled city near the edge of the great Sahara Desert, where camel trains and jumbo jets now meet as viable links in the modern international transport system. In my time, however, there was just an R.A.F. base at Kano and an air strip at Kaduna where later I went on a course. The 'English teacher' not only looked after the men's welfare, including running a canteen for them, but also taught them the fundamental words of command in the British Army and showed them, by means of diagrams in the sandy soil around the parade ground, how to 'left flanker' and 'right flanker' in the platoon attack drill. He also hinted to me that I might learn a little of their Hausa language and sometimes, in the comparative cool of the evening, he would come to my gidda. This gidda consisted of a roundel hut with a thatched roof, a little veranda which was 'wired in' against mosquito attacks, and a mines and explosives store for which I was responsible, attached to the back.

Fred Katsina, my batman, turned out to be a gem. He appeared to be no older than I was but told me that he had several children. "I not sure how old I am, Sah" he confided, "but I have two wives and I make allotment to my first wife called Philomena". He had spent some time in the city of Enugu and therefore knew the customs of the white man. This proved most useful for he could liaise with the 'English teacher' when I had trouble with the interpretation of battalion orders to my men.

After a hot and sweaty four weeks on the parade ground and the assault course, we were ordered to march our men up to the firing ranges some mile and a half across the valley from the camp. We had to cross the railway line, pass the mission school where (apart from the most delicious squash made by the boys from oranges, lemons, limes and grapefruit growing locally), we attended the mission church on Sundays, and march up the hill past a native compound serving the Public Works department European settlement to an area much like a vast English common in the dry season but now with the rains starting, covered with grass which could spring up as much as 18" in one night.

The butts had been located in a shallow depression below some bare rock boulders which were so hot in the day that you could not touch them, and we knew that snakes and iguanas basked in this area.

The rifle firing continued without incident except that it was very unwise for any instructor to walk in front of the firing point before *all* the soldiers' rifles had been inspected and seen to be unloaded. The trouble started for me on our second day out when we were ordered to teach the men the art of firing a grenade from a discharger cup attached to a 303 rifle. The soldier had to reverse his rifle, screw on the discharger cup, load the charged cartridge, take the safety pin out of the grenade while holding the release lever tightly, place the grenade in the cup, aim the rifle at an angle to the horizon with the rifle butt on the ground, then pull the trigger. Imagine yourself to be a young man from a bush village who has never even travelled to a native town, let alone a big British Army camp, and you will understand how confusing such an operation can be. Thus I was faced with the task of demolishing the many 'blinds' which lay in the long grass at the end of the firing range. My training as a Signals officer had not included an explosives course and I had to rely on the few weeks of Infantry instruction I had received during my officer training in England. I don't know whether I was more scared of the creepy-crawlies in the grass or of the detonators and gun cotton which I had to place against each unexploded grenade before ignition took place, but having 'blown' one of the offenders, I'm darn sure that no snakes remained on my patch!

Some weeks before this experience, a squad of inmates from the local prison had been detailed to cut the long grass adjacent to the ranges.

The Africans would line up and then advance with their crude scythes, moving from right to left in a rhythmic sequence, their bodies glistening with sweat in the hot humid air.

Unfortunately, some careless soldier had failed to report the non-explosion of a plastic grenade and an unsuspecting prisoner had cut the wretched thing in half, blowing himself to smithereens in the process!

The culprit was never found, of course, but the soldiery lost their popularity for a long time to come, especially in the native village nearby which was mostly inhabited by the women dependents of the prisoners.

The rifle with its discharger cup did have one rather interesting secondary use, however. Our fiendish Burma sergeant had patented his own method of projecting a rope-line across a river or gulley by fixing the rope end to a dummy grenade and firing it in the normal way from the discharger cup. We organised several successful river-crossing exercises using this device and our African soldiers would chuckle delightedly when they saw the rope spring out like a snake and land on the distant bank. Ultimate success did, of course, rely on a rifle aimed accurately to lodge the rope around the branch of a tree on the far side and there were many crestfallen soldiers when the rope fell back into the water to no effect.

Part of the basic training for the Africans took place on the assault course and most of the men were very good at swarming up ropes and nets. There was always a queue to be first to traverse the rope across the chasm, and great shouts of laughter if one unfortunate soldier was too heavy and broke the branch around which the rope was attached so that he fell into the water with a great splash.

Since there were very few Europeans in a West African battalion, mess nights were taken very seriously and rank had to be observed very correctly. Our Colonel had been through the Somalian campaign of 1942 where the ritual in the mess had not differed much from that of Khartoum half a century before. Consequently, the port was still passed to the left of the great man despite the fact that we were located in a mess hut with a tin roof and wooden walls. Our food was cooked by Africans in the old colonial style and we enjoyed the groundnut stews with curry, banana and shredded coconut, followed by a large natural fruit salad definitely home grown! After the meal, officers would gather around the Colonel, some to drink Van der Hum from South Africa, others whisky, to discuss the day's happenings and swap amusing stories of our charming but sometimes exasperating trainee African soldiers.

The second-in-command, a Major Brown, had served in the W.A.F.F. since pre-war days and thus qualified to be described as a "coaster". He was short and thick-set with a weather beaten face and a very red nose. "Nothing much else to do but drink in this God-forsaken dump", he used to complain. He lived for his home leave and the occasional trip to S. Africa. We knew that he had an African mistress tucked away in Lagos, but since he rarely had a chance to visit the capital, he used to seek out the local village ladies and return to camp blind drunk in the early hours of the morning, usually waking us up as he bumped along the verandah to his quarters.

Our company commanders and their deputies were mostly wartime soldiers like us, but one or two of them emulated our 'coaster' to the extent of inviting some of the more nubile young African girls to their quarters if given the opportunity.

Each subaltern commanded a platoon and he was supported by a British Sergeant as well as an African counterpart.

The European N.C.O.'s had their own mess, of course, and the officers exchanged visits from time to time. African girls would often be present on these occasions and Henry White had to be physically held back by the rest of us one evening when he took a fancy to my Sergeant's latest girl friend.

The sixteen weeks of initial training were soon over and then the rains really came down.

CHAPTER SIX

In Darkest Africa

Tropical rain in the Gombe forest acts as a trigger to the growth of all those creepy crawlies that we dream about in our northern childhood. Those beautiful butterflies disappeared and slow-worms, over half a metre long, appeared in the outdoor earth closets. Scorpions played beneath the camp lights, and we checked our spare clothes and boots to ensure that they and the poisonous spiders were not hiding in them. Snakes were attracted to the warmth of our huts, and the high humidity produced bugs, beetles and mosquitoes in their thousands.

We suffered from sweat rash, and the Burma sergeant reminded us that we would have to cope with the leeches as well when we reached the Arakan.

My personal responsibility was to keep the explosives and ammunition dry and, more important, the antiquated back-pack wireless sets which went on the blink in the dry weather let alone in the torrential rain! I got my platoon digging rainwater trenches and repairing holes in tin roofs or renewing grass thatch on the soldiers' giddas.

The grass around the camp grew 18" high in a night, and the tentacles of jungle creepers seemed to penetrate into our very souls. The Africans from the northern plains were as bemused as we British, but the soldiers who had been recruited locally took it in their stride. They were Yoruba men from the villages in the Western province and many spoke English since they were accustomed to bringing produce from their villages down into the big town's 'mammy' markets.

In those days, each town or area had a British District Officer who, with an Assistant D.O., and staff looked after matters concerning the Colonial administration, Justice and Police. As most of the A.D.O.'s had been called up, however, British Army lieutenants stationed in that particular area were detached from their regiments to assist the D.O. when necessary. I was asked by our D.O. to help with the local recruiting drive towards the end of 1944.

We were still short of African soldiers to make up the battalion strength and so one day I was instructed to pay a call on our local Yoruba dignatory or King who lived in a rather run-down palace just outside the African town. I wore my full dress uniform with Sam Browne belt and borrowed the District Officer's staff car for the occasion.

The driver pulled up outside a courtyard thronged with jostling people who, I supposed, were also seeking audience with the great man. It was hot and humid and whole families grouped round their spokesman, and dogs barked as the children played with them.

Across the courtyard which was stockaded, I saw a series of mud-walled huts linked along the front by an enormous multi-stepped verandah leading into the largest of them. I could see that this was the throne room, for carpets led the eye to the great chair on which sat the most wizened little man I had ever laid eyes upon! His court were grouped around him, clad in colourful robes, while the Alake himself had a distinctive sash, an elaborate bejewelled headdress and was smoking a cheroot.

"Sanu - welcome, my friend." He motioned me to a chair by his side and an aide offered me a drink of African beer.

"You have come from the D.O. to ask about further recruits for His Majesty's army?" "Yes, sir, that is correct. A new battalion of the Nigerian Regiment is being formed to do service in Burma and it is to replace a similar unit which will return home from the Arakan Front after gallant service."

"That is good news" croaked the old man, "we shall have to consult with the village headmen to see what can be done and then I will contact the honourable District Commissioner myself."

The Alake nodded his head and I knew that it was time to go. Smart salutes were required, about turn and away to the car I went.

I shall never forget that strange interview with one of the last remaining native representatives of the British Colonial administration, for Nigeria was to become independent within a short time.

"You seem to have done a good job on our friend, the Alake" said the D.C. "We have the go-ahead to recruit in the villages around here, so report to your colonel and fix up transport to take a team of British N.C.O.'s along to demonstrate the 'advantages' of being a soldier in the Royal West African Frontier Force."

"You mean the good grub and a shilling a day to see the world bit, Sir!"

"Now, don't be cynical, lad - most of these Africans long to get away from their villages and earn a bit of their own money. I doubt whether my people will ever settle down to farming again after their return from foreign parts - the soldiers have learned a hell of a lot out in India and Burma, including a bit of pride in themselves! They'll probably clean out their villages and demand motorbikes and bars for entertainment."

"O.K. Sir, I get the drift and I'll do what I can to recruit the numbers we require."

It didn't take many days to organise a three truck sortie

to the villages to the west of us. I took my British sergeant with the name of Wince, two African corporals and a section of our soldiers who would carry out drill in front of the village young men. Sergeant Wince would enrol any likely lads and pay them the King's shilling. After a drive along a rather dusty road we arrived at the village of Djinja. Not a soul in sight, but since we had to report to the local headman before setting up shop anyhow, this didn't disconcert us unduly.

"Where does the headman live, Sergeant, any ideas?"

"Supposed to be located in a hut right at the centre of the village, Sir."

"Ah! That looks like it" I said. The headman had been told to expect us so I was a little surprised at the lack of enthusiasm. We approached the hut only to find it empty.

"Where the hell has he got to?" I exclaimed.

"I've looked around the huts, Sir, and there's no-one about."

"Damn - you know, we've frightened them off! Let's go to the next village on the list and see if we have any better luck."

"Right, Sir" said the Sergeant, "the men are still in the trucks so I'll give the order to move off".

We trundled on down the road which had now deteriorated into a track with dense jungle either side of us, and suddenly we were in yet another of those vast clearings in the Gombe Forest. Here, the villagers of Asayin greeted us with cheers and handclaps as they clustered round our trucks. Their ranks suddenly parted and the headman emerged in all his finery. Not to be compared with the Alake, he nonetheless possessed a colourful pair of shorts and a khaki jacket obviously 'won' from a soldier. Nothing on his feet, but beads round his neck and a wicked smile!

"Sanu my gidda" he said, and beckoned me to his hut. I

told Sergeant Wince to stay with the soldiers and followed the headman. I staggered a bit as the stench in the interior of the hut hit me, but I realised that it was only the smell of spilt beer and the entrails of a chicken, the carcase of which had been eaten clean.

"I be headman of this village, Sah" he said, "I find you good soldiers for His Majesty's army as before. Do you have my 'dash'?" I hadn't been ready for such a proposition and stammered something about only having the King's shilling!

"Must have 'dash' else no soldiers, Sah."

At that I marched out in high dudgeon and told Sergeant Wince to set up our demonstration parade to see whether we could recruit any men without the help of the headman.

"Get on parade" shouted the Sergeant to the African soldiers who, until this moment, were still sitting in the trucks. Much clatter of boots and rifle butts but quite a smart turn-out for all that. Arms drill was demonstrated and at its completion there was much clapping and cheering once again.

"Now, who is brave enough to volunteer for service with these gallant soldiers" called one of the African corporals, in their own dialect. No-one came forward but there was more exclamation and cheering.

I took the corporal to one side and ordered him to tell the villagers about the good army food and the chance to see the big cities of other countries. Still no reaction and we could see the headman moving about amongst the young men of the village. Obviously he was telling them to do nothing until he had made a good 'arrangement' with the white officer.

I had no funds for such bribery and therefore decided to call it a day and return to camp for further instructions.

The Colonel was vastly amused when he heard my

story.

"You haven't been away from home for long, have you, David?"

"No, Sir, but I don't like bribery."

"All African people like a 'dash', you know - been going on for generations."

"Then what shall we do next, Sir" I said. "We must go back to the D.O. and ask his opinion, Lieutenant England. I'll phone him and get his reaction."

I returned to my regular duties and heard nothing more for a few days. Then I was called to the C.O.'s office where the Colonel told me to proceed once again to the village with my convoy, seek out the headman and deliver a crate to him before giving the army demonstration. They are going to bribe him with beer, I thought, but what's that to me - not my business any more! The crate was enormous, however, and we had some trouble getting it into the hut.

I carried on with my parade and to my surprise we had no less than seven volunteers to join the army. Sergeant Wince paid them their shiny shillings and they boarded the truck quite happily. I was just about to board myself when the headman rushed up to me and shook me by the hand many times.

"What a number one present is this bath I received from the great King George" he said. "I now bath myself and all my wives in my gidda, Sanu", and with that, he disappeared into the hut where we could hear splashing and raucous laughter.

I was never quite sure just how willingly those men did join the Army, and I wondered what extra pressures were put on them by the unscrupulous elders of the villages. I had to admit that the Army did give them a permanent job and each soldier was to make a marriage allotment to one of his many wives, and thus fill the family coffers. I had many amusing interviews with members of my platoon to negotiate the thorny pitfalls of the favoured wife!

Because I was in command of the Signals and Engineering platoon at this time, I had some of the more intelligent men to deal with. Some of the brightest ones came from the Eastern province, many years later to be re-named Biafra. They were Ibo's, mostly Christian and speaking English. I was told to teach them the rudiments of wireless communication using the old Army 18 set which had become obsolete in the European theatre of war by this time. I have already mentioned that the rains played havoc with these battery-operated sets still equipped with thermionic valves and every time I managed to persuade my operators to speak into the microphone, the set would go dead. "There must be a 'ju-ju' in it", they would say!

The men were more at home with telephone communications for they could *see* the cable which they excitedly disgorged from the metal drums mounted on a 15 cwt. truck.

"Aba" they would exclaim, "there be only one wire to screw on to *two* terminals - where is the other one?" When I told them that the signal was completed when the second terminal was connected to an *earth* pin to travel through the ground, they suspected a 'Ju-ju' once again. At least the telephone worked, so confidence was finally restored.

At last we had trained the soldiers sufficiently to carry out simple battalion exercises in the jungle around the camp.

The Infantry platoons were deployed in sections, one covering the other two, and they practised 'left and right flankers' as they called it. As my platoon could hardly lay lines in the thick scrub, we endeavoured to maintain wireless communications between battalion and the company headquarters but, as inevitably happens, we had to rely on runners to deliver written messages between the advancing units.

No live firing could be allowed at this stage but the thunderflashes were exploding all over the Gombe Forest! At one point we were able to practise firing the rope from the discharger cup on the rifle, since our advance took us across a wide stream which a few weeks before would have been a bone dry gulley.

After we returned to camp, both African soldiers and their British Officers and N.C.O.'s were given a rest period and Henry and I volunteered to get up two cricket teams with the active support of our Colonel. Great fun was had by all with the Africans looking on and cheering. The Colonel was so enthusiastic that we challenged our sister battalion stationed on the outskirts of Ibadan, an enormous sprawling town situated some miles north of us, to a one-day match. Our pitch was to be used, since we had inherited a natural flat clearing quite equal to the size of an English town cricket ground. The opposition were to travel down the only tarmac road existing in Western Nigeria at that time, a distance of some 40 miles. Dropped catches on both sides off many skied mishits dictated an honourable draw.

About this time I was asked to attend a sapper course at the Engineers School at a pleasant place up country. The town was called Kaduna and was reached by train. After many hours of travel, we came to the great river Niger at a place called Jebba, famous for the explorer Mungo Park, who eventually lost his life to local tribesmen. To my surprise, we crossed the river on a modern steel bridge and my first view of the Northern Territory was of a coal mine with its winding-tower protruding above the forest just a few hundred yards from the muddy north bank of the river. One could feel the presence of the crocodiles and the humidity seemed to engulf us as we stepped out onto the station platform. After the engine had been replaced, the train set off again and after an hour or so, the jungle gave way to open savanna with its dried up water holes and red-brown scrub, and we were clear of the Gombe Forest. Now we were free of the dreaded tsetse fly pest and we could see the gazelle fleeing the sound of the steam train as it wound its way up onto the plateau on which Kaduna stood.

Kaduna was clean and well laid out, certainly under the influence of earlier railmen, and it boasted a race course. The Engineering School was located near the airstrip to the west of the town and I was impressed, on my arrival, to see two chameleons slowly but deliberately climbing the wire mesh on the verandah of the Officers' Mess. As I clanked up the wooden steps, these interesting creatures changed colour with fright and merged into the background.

"Oh, there you are" said the Adjutant "come in and make yourself at home." I hadn't received such a welcome since I had been commissioned more than a year before, and I knew that I was going to like these folk and decided to throw myself into the spirit of the course, which was to teach me how to demolish railway lines and bridges and how to clear suspect buildings and telegraph installations of booby-traps. The instructors were surprised to have a Royal Corps of Signals Officer on their course, and it was not long before they asked me to take my turn on the army 22 wireless set to contact the D.C.3 supply Dakotas and give them landing instructions, wind directions etc.

This brought me into contact with the R.A.F. for the first time since officer training days, and we had some amusing mess evenings with the crews during their weekly visits. I would like to have attended this course before taking the African soldiers on the grenade firing ranges at

Abeokuta for I soon realised that I had been fortunate not to have blown myself up during my very amateur sorties into the long grass on the infantry ranges.

I did wonder what use much of our work would be in the jungle ravines of the Arakan in Burma, but 'mine was not to reason why'!

I was loth to return south at the end of the 4 week course for I realised that our mobilisation was imminent, and, sure enough, there was great activity when I arrived at my unit's camp just outside Ibadan.

Our palm tree-lined camp was flanked by a reservoir in which lived a tame crocodile. We never tried to make friends with him although he *was* sacred, but some intrepid officers did go swimming, having arranged for lookouts to be posted, equipped with binoculars, just in case this kelpie decided to swim up to have a look at the strange white smooth-skinned mosters.

Some Ibadans at this time still worshipped the Thunder God and revered sacred creatures although the Moslems dominated, with the Copts and Christians following in their wake.

It is interesting to note that not long after we left, the University College of Nigeria was founded in this great native city rather than in the capital city, Lagos.

Henry White was nowhere to be seen and I soon learned from the adjutant that his forthright cockiness or confident initiative, to put it officially, had earned him a place in the advance party which had already boarded a ship en route for India to prepare for the reception of our battalion.

We were to follow in a few weeks but in the meantime there was apparently a job for me in Lagos before we moved off.

The C.O. summoned me and told me that I was to take my platoon, in transport provided, to Ikeja Airport just to the north of Lagos, and to await orders to proceed to Lagos central prison in order to provide a riot squad in support of the civilian police. There had been friction between the north and the south of the country, partly stirred up by certain politicians and partly caused because the cattle farmers in the north would not send meat to the south due to dissatisfaction with the treatment they were receiving from the central government in Lagos. Rioting was thus expected because of food shortages. Added to this, two steam engines had been deliberately derailed from the single track main line just below Ikeja by members of the Liberation Front who were, by this time, agitating for Nigerian Independence. The war in Europe had just come to an end but we hardly noticed the reports of the celebrations for V.E. day 1945 in U.K. since we realised that our battle for S.E. Asia still lay ahead of us.

It was true that units of the West African 81st Division were just about to be repatriated after fine service in the Arakan, and thus to many Nigerians the war was over.

Our unit which was part of the newly formed 82nd West African Division, was designated to replace these men in Burma and we were pleased to be near to a big city, perhaps for the last time, before our fight with the Japs.

Sergeant Wince and I were billeted in a pleasant Public Works Department house with the friendly little Gecko lizards chasing flies over the ceiling, in the European quarter of Lagos, and we stood duty in the prison with two sections of soldiers turn and turn about. I was able to visit the European Colonial Club for the first time, enjoy a bath and eat in a civilised manner. We had many games of snooker while we waited for some action - but in the end sense prevailed, the engines were winched back on to the track, and the meat trains rolled once again. The civilian police were able to cope with the troublemakers who were never allowed to form into organised gangs.

It is interesting that the big city should offer up one of the strangest and most bizarre situations during my time in West Africa.

During our time in Lagos, it was necessary to ask the soldiers to erect barbed wire barricades, and during one hot and sweaty morning's work, I noticed that some of the men were not wearing their regulation shirts with reinforced shoulder pieces. Suddenly, one of the soldiers fell, chest downwards, and appeared to be digging into the hard earth with both his legs and arms. By the time I collected the African Sergeant and had reached the man, he was quite still and appeared to be unconscious. "Is he ill, Sergeant?"

"I do not know, Sah, but he is a Munchiman and he make Ju-Ju."

"A Ju-Ju; what do you mean?"

"Well, Sah, it is very hot and maybe the soldier does not like his work and as a protest he has made a spell and gone into a trance."

"Good Lord, can he do it just like that, without any preparation?"

"Yes, Sah, and we can do nothing until one of his own tribe release him from his Ju-Ju."

"Well, get hold of a Munchi N.C.O. pronto and tell him to talk to the chap" I said with some irritation.

"Right, Sah, I will look" and with that the Sergeant hurried off to find help.

A most impressive corporal reported to me after about ten minutes during which time the prostrate soldier hadn't moved a muscle. The corporal had deep-set cuts on either side of his face, received at the time of his initiation to manhood, and he was bearded. He saluted smartly and asked what was required of him.

"Can you do something to get this man on his feet again?"

"Yes, Sah" said the corporal, "but it will be necessary to light a small fire on his back before I can free him."

"A fire!" I said. "That's a bit drastic, isn't it?"

"No, Sah - he will understand nothing else - it is his tribal custom."

"O.K., you had better get on with it then" I said.

The corporal saluted and went up to the soldier, placed a few leaves on his back and lit them with a match.

Almost at once, the man responded, tottered to his feet, picked up the roll of barbed wire which he had originally dropped and went about his duty as if nothing had happened!

I, of course, reported this incident to the Adjutant at District Headquarters and, to my surprise, he bellowed with laughter.

"Didn't anyone tell you about these extraordinary African customs, England? Come round to see me one evening when you are off duty and I'll tell you a bit about these mysterious Ju-Ju customs."

"Thanks, Sir" I said. "It would be most interesting to learn more about the ability of these people to will themselves into a trance."

We didn't stay long at the Adjutant's house that evening, as it happened, for he had arranged to take me and a few others to an African club on the outskirts of Lagos where, he said, all would be revealed.

"No good just telling you chaps about this Ju-Ju business - you had better see for yourselves."

The club was situated on the edge of the lagoon and to approach it we had to walk along a swampy track through the mango swamps and palm trees, which were hung with gaudy coloured electric light bulbs. A wooden dance floor had been placed in front of some thatched huts, and African music was being played by drummers and other musicians. The so-called stage was lit with smoky oil lamps and it was altogether a most exotic setting.

We were offered beer by a most attractive African girl of about 18 years old, dressed in a white blouse with many brightly coloured beads and bangles and a very short skirt, no shoes or stockings. She was a resident hostess and dancer from the Yoruba tribe. We were told that she had been born in a jungle village and had managed to get away to the big city when she was 14 years old to live with an old aunt. She was sent to work as a servant-girl to a European family where she had learned good English. Too late for secondary school and an office life in Lagos, she had settled for club life at 16. She was particularly attractive to the club owner because while dancing to drum music, she could work herself into a Ju-Ju trance.

"Do the tribal witch doctors still put spells on the villagers, and force them into carrying out these mystic rituals?" I heard myself ask.

"I'm not so sure about that" replied the Adjutant, "but as you already know, it is mighty useful to go into a trance if you don't want to do something unpleasant, or if you feel like withdrawing your labour or striking! Also, Western people sometimes whip themselves up into a religious fervour, which almost comes to the same thing, doesn't it?"

We all agreed and settled in to watch the African girl work herself up into a trance using an erotic dance routine which included the divestment of all her clothes other than her beads and bangles!

I had heard of hypnotists inducing such a trance in receptive subjects back at home and I knew that the medical profession frowned on this practice which had been successful in helping patients suffering from nervous tension.

Our doctors could not accept the Svengali-power transferred to the hypnotist whilst the subject was in the trance.

Quite different in Africa, it appeared, and we all cheered the curvaceous girl when the Night Club boss snapped his fingers to wake her from her frenzy.

Soon after this incident our mobilisation orders arrived and we returned to Ikeja to kit up for the long sea trip to Akyab just over the Burma border with India, now Pakistan.

CHAPTER SEVEN

Mobilisation

To mobilise a battalion of African troops in the 1940's was quite some task and we were summoned to the Colonel's 'O' group many times before the great day of embarkation eventually came.

Most of my men had never seen the sea before, let alone sailed in a ship. Realising this, I recruited the aid of my 'English teacher' and, with sketches and diagrams, we organised a routine for the soldiers once they had filed up the gangways of the Orient Princess and proceeded to their mess decks, converted from the cargo holds. Our ship had been a passenger-cargo carrier in peacetime and thus the hundred or so cabins were all located on the upper decks adjacent to the officers' quarters near to the bridge.

My soldiers had mostly come from remote villages and they were horrified to find that they were confined to a steel 'prison'. We had to train them in the use of modern flush loos or 'heads' as the Navy calls them. We had, of course, organised tin bucket-tip showers for them in the camps on shore so they made a bee-line for the ship's modern pipe-fed equivalents whenever it was their turn.

The 'English teacher himself had been puzzled when, at my platoon briefing parade, I told the men that we should be first sailing to the West round the bulge of Africa and into the Mediterranean, then through the Suez Canal to the East!

"Why we do that, Sah?" he said. "When we go for Egypt, we take a lorry to Lake Chad and then over the sand desert sometimes with camels."

I explained that we would need so many lorries and camels to transport a battalion that a ship was the only practical way of travelling!

The sirens sounded and the ship cast off from Appapa wharf to sail down Lagos Lagoon for the open sea and then to Takoradi, the modern Bauxite port of the Gold Coast (now Ghana) where we were to pick up a battalion from our sister West African country, also *en route* for the Arakan in Burma.

News from the forgotten army of Bill Slim's in S.E.A.C. was good and there had been advances on the central front, but only slight progress on Arakan front. Perhaps it would be our men who would push through and join up with the British and Indian troops who had already taken the port of Rangoon.

We continued our training while sitting in groups on the open decks in super weather accompanied by flying fish, dolphins and, of course, the giant sea turtles along the West African coast.

It was good to be in European waters once again, and after a brief call at colourful Algiers with its attractive white Moslem-style apartment buildings blending with the tall towers of the Mosques, we sailed serenely along the North African coast in sight of the beaches most of the way.

There was much excitement as we approached the long mole of Port Said with its lighthouse and the entrance to the Suez Canal. A certain amount of nostalgia from we Europeans for, with the war finished in this part of the world, it was hard now to be travelling *East* instead of *West*. The ship tied up in Port Said just to take on fresh water and victuals, although the Africans had brought much of their own special food, Yams and Cassava, with them.

We received our signal from the Canal Authority to proceed down the waterway and we realised that we were actually on our way to the Far East. Floating down the

Canal in a large ship is quite an experience since there is flat desert on either side with, of course, the sandhill escarpments some distance to the West, guarding the road to Cairo. A ship in the desert!

After some hours, we cleared Port Suez and entered the Red Sea. Now for it, we thought, but suddenly there was great excitement on the bridge and the Chief Officer burst out on to the wing bridge to tell us that the Americans had dropped a second atomic bomb, this time on Nagasaki, in Japan, and that the Japs were sueing for peace. We were beside ourselves with delight! Some hours later we heard the news that we were to return to Port Said to complete our service in Egypt and *not* Burma!

This was to be our second view of Port Said, where, we had learned at school, East meets West. Having spent over a year in Nigeria, however, the gilt was off the gingerbread and we had become quite used to the sickly stench of open drains and the smell of food cooked over a smoky fire in the open air. When we finally disembarked, we did become aware of the subtle difference between equatorial Africa and the Arabic Middle East. Egypt, after all, had witnessed many dynasties before the Romans took over their land, and much longer than we Britons. They still used their age-old river boats called feluccas on all their canals and waterways and it was fascinating just to watch them glide past the Navy's fussy picket boats and mechanically propelled lighters plying between the cargo boats and the many jetties.

Our ship actually tied up alongside, and before we came down the gangplank we had bought gifts and fruit from the Egyptians operating the famous Bum Boats on the canal side of the vessel. Small boys dived for pennies just

as they had done for a century or more in all the tropical ports serving the British Empire.
Of course at this time we had no idea that our Empire was going to collapse within 25 years!

In a way we had been looking forward to landing in India before going to Burma or beyond, for we had heard that the Indians had already insisted that their independence must come in the next year or so, and we wanted to see for ourselves why they should think themselves advanced enough to cope with the thorny problems of peace which reports from the Conference at Yalta had indicated. After all, they were split between two different religions and customs far more complex than those between the English, Welsh and Scots. Within a few weeks of landing in this country which had also tolerated the British for half a century, we came to know that we were no longer wanted and that our so-called allies were hell bent to get us out!

Thus, as we drove through the streets of Port Said that day, we had some foreboding of the future - our stay here might not be any picnic. The streets were quaint and many of them overhung with wooden balconies. Some of the stores were modern and we would have given a lot to spend that day window-shopping since we had been away from such places for a long time.

The town had been developed by the French while they were building the Canal and on the Sinai bank, Port Fouad contained some delightful villas and a good beach on the Mediterranean coast.

The European Canal Company's lease, negotiated by Disraeli, was fast running out as we were forcibly told when we eventually did visit this fascinating port while on day leave.

Our trucks rumbled on through the streets and out onto a good tarmac road to Ismailia, a large Egyptian town at the junction of the Sweet Water Canal linking the Nile to Lake Timsah. Over the bridge we soon came upon the Great Bitter Lake, which we had already seen from the ship, and it looked quite different from the land.

The convoy halted and the officers were called to an 'O' group for our orders. To our dismay, we learned from the Colonel that since we had not been expected, we would have to draw tents and equipment from the local Quartermaster's store and make our own camp just off the road and under the sandhills forming the Northern extent of the Arabian Desert. On the credit side, we were only four miles from the regular camp at Fayid and the British officers and sergeants would be able to use the Officers' Club and Sergeants' Mess while off duty. What bliss to get back amongst our own people again, we thought.

The African troops under command would not be allowed to move from camp, however, until they had become accustomed to the wicked ways of the Middle East! This was, in no time at all, to cause much trouble since the Africans had no womenfolk with them and the bare open desert was quite alien to the Gombe Forest and the scrub-covered plains to which they were accustomed.

For the first week we were more than occupied in erecting tents, man-handling stores and whitewashing stones which were placed to denote our parade ground and track to the tarmac road.

Our major, who mysteriously appeared on horseback, and our African regimental sergeant-major had a field-day. Back to peacetime with a vengeance, we thought. The sergeant-major was a fine figure of a man - well over 6 feet in height with rugged complexion and goatee beard. He had fought in Eritrea and Somaliland with medals to prove it, and, shunning ammunition boots, polished his feet with Kiwi boot polish to a brilliant shine!

Being in charge of the Signals and Engineering platoon I

was too tired at the end of the day to do anything but flop down on my camp bed. My ever faithful batman (promoted from 'Boy-Boy' in West Africa) Fred Katsina, was marvellous and scrounged mugs of tea and buns from the Officers' Mess-tent a few hundred yards away - which saved me socialising with the others who were also overtired and thus argumentative.

The soldiers were becoming quite efficient and soon ran a telephone cable from our H.Q. tent to the distribution point half a mile away on the road. It was good to meet with the Royal Corps of Signals' officer in charge of our district, for we had friends in common from our days in England, while training with British Divisions which were not used by General Montgomery for the Second Front in June 1944.

"Why don't you apply for transfer to Middle East Signals now the war is over?" he said. "The older men will be demobbed soon and we are going to be short of staff." I told him that nothing would please me better but that I felt loyalty to my Africans who the 'big White King' had thought to uproot from their homelands to fight in Burma and now found themselves in this alien land.

As there was no active work for us to do, we were instructed to organise training parades for the men. A lot of square-bashing but also the odd sortie up into the sandhills to do platoon training. Our signallers didn't like this work at all and persuaded the Major to let us blow up an imaginary railway line and build a rope bridge over an imaginary chasm. All a bit tame after the training for Burma. I managed to escape with another subaltern to the Officers' Club at Fayid. This was luxury! A swim in the very salty lake where one can float without moving hands or feet, followed by a shower and a cool drink on the balcony which stretched out over the lake, was bliss. The sun was hot and although the temperature was in the 90°s it was a dry heat; such a contrast after our 80% humidity in Nigeria.

Some of the regular officers had their yachts on moorings around the Club and went off on voyages to Ismailia and to Port Suez to the South. Quite like the Solent in peacetime!

One day, I was asked to organise a three truck convoy to collect some advance equipment from Ismailia, routed on the little used secondary road to the West of Fayid. I put an African sergeant in charge of the drivers and their escorts for their first sortie under their own steam in the Middle East. The escorts were armed, of course, but I was ordered to issue only five rounds of ammunition to each of them, since no trouble was anticipated. The convoy set out in the morning and was due back by 16.00 hours local time. I had plenty of training work to carry out and so forgot all about the convoy.

It was about 16.30 hours when I was called to the Adjutant's tent and reminded that the sergeant in charge of the convoy had not reported in. Since he had no radio I was told to go and look for him. It sounded rather suspicious since all three trucks couldn't have broken down - so I took four men and a corporal, with rifles and ammunition and I carried my revolver just in case.

We followed the convoy route and after about six miles came upon the trucks. No sign of life, and as we got close I realised that all the wheels and tyres were missing from the rear vehicle. I ordered my men to dismount and spread out to look for their missing comrades and possible attackers. No sign of either, so they had either been kidnapped or had 'gone to bush' as West African soldiers always put it! What should I do now! - we didn't have walkie-talkies in those days, so I couldn't contact the camp although I had left word that if I didn't return within two hours, a party should set out to look for me.

I inspected our vehicles and found that everything movable had been taken away even down to the distributor leads and plugs! Who had done this and where were our men? Before taking any action at all I had to know what had happened to the soldiers. If they had been kidnapped, I would have to contact Headquarters for instructions since ten to one the robbers were Egyptian citizens and therefore allies. On the other hand, perhaps a gang had come down from Syria or Palestine. There had been marauders in the desert lands since time immemorial and I could not prejudge. For a start I could make a search around the immediate area of desert in the hope that our men *had* 'gone to bush' and were hiding behind the undulating sandhills. There was a certain amount of scrub grass in this part of the canal zone and the whole area away from the road looked like a giant gravel pit.

"Spread out over the ground" I told my escort, "Load your rifles and keep them at the ready but don't shoot at anybody unless I give the command - understand?"

"Yes, sah" answered the corporal who spoke reasonable English.

We found nothing after searching for about an hour and so I decided to remain by the trucks with three men and send the corporal and a driver back to camp to report the men and vehicle accessories missing. I gave the corporal a message to my captain, requesting that a signal should be sent to all neighbouring units and the local police to discover whether any of our men had reported in. In the meantime I placed my men in positions of defence and told them to keep a good watch for any movements either on the road or around the vehicles. I hoped that other British Army vehicles would be using this road but by this time it was 17.15 hours and darkness would be upon us within an hour. All was quiet for about half an hour and then, to my amazement, I saw a small camel train silhouetted against a sandhill about 500 yards away. "Stand to" I said to my men, "and see that your rifles are loaded but with the safety catches on!" Were the robbers returning to the scene or were these Egyptian traders going about their legitimate business? I waited under cover until they were 200 yards away and then saw that the three riders cradled shot guns in their arms. They circled round our positions and it was obvious that they were up to no good. Then one of the men came forward and dismounted by one of the derelict trucks while the other two remained mounted on their camels.

"Now!" I said to two of the soldiers. "Go round the back of the mounted men and order them to drop their guns. The other men and I will cover your action. No-one is to fire unless I tell you to do so. Keep your safety catches on - we don't want an unnecessary incident in this part of the world." I edged nearer to the dismounted camel man and managed to knock his gun out of his hand since we had the advantage of surprise. His reaction was rapid and he jumped away from my grasp and disappeared round the truck. "Damn, he's got away" I thought. I was concentrating so hard that I only vaguely heard shots beyond me. Someone had fired his rifle without an order and he had winged the robber on foot. The other camel-men turned and retreated in great surprise. Our soldiers could not contain themselves, broke cover and ran towards the fallen figure who was clothed in a filthy white garment and was bleeding from the leg.

"My God" I thought "Now I'm in trouble. This man is undoubtedly a villain but he is probably an Egyptian national and I have wounded an ally!" I hoped he might speak English so that we could discover what had happened to our men and equipment. No such luck! The hapless Arab merely groaned and turned his eyes to Allah!

We used a field dressing on his leg and stopped the bleeding.

"Who fired that shot?" I demanded.

"I sah" said a shaky African soldier. "Der safety catch comes off in my hand and I shoot by mistake."

"At least you were accurate" I said, "but you disobeyed an order and you will be put on a charge when you get back to camp."

I felt sorry for the lad for he had saved the day, so far as I was concerned, and we had a prisoner to question when we got to H.Q.

By this time dusk had fallen and I wondered where the corporal had got to - we had no mobile transport until he returned. Fortunately, he arrived soon after to tell me that our men from the truck convoy had not yet been found, but that a full scale recovery operation was being mounted. In the meantime we were instructed to return to camp. "Unfortunately, Corporal" I said "We have a wounded Arab to be dealt with and I think that he knows what happened to our convoy." The soldiers loaded the Arab into our truck - not too gently - and we returned to camp.

All hell was let loose there and Barny, our newly appointed Captain, told me that I should have to answer to the Major when he arrived back at the camp.

In the meantime we had to take the Arab to the camp casualty centre for treatment to his leg. This was not possible until he had been stripped of his foul clothing and bathed. He still said nothing and it was obvious that we should have to find a local interpreter before he could be questioned.

This was the Major's job, and after a curt rebuke for making so much trouble, I was told to "get the hell out of here and see to your men." It was not the moment to ask about any progress in finding the missing convoy personnel but the next morning we were told that our soldiers had been surprised by men on camels who had obstructed their progress on the road, bringing them to a halt and when they saw shotguns pointing at them, they had literally 'gone to bush' behind some sandhills. They had stayed put until the robbers had left and had then made their way to the main Ismailia-Suez road where they had been picked up by another army unit. On their return they were put in the guard tent pending the inevitable enquiry.

I was making myself as scarce as possible but I was naturally anxious to know if the interpreter had got any information out of the captured Arab. It seemed, however, that he had been whisked away to area H.Q. at Fayid, and it was weeks before the full story broke. It was at the Court of Inquiry that I learned the full details.

Apparently, the riff-raff of the Nile Delta area had learned of the needs of the new illegal Jewish immigrants to Palestine and had decided to supply them from British Army stores and units. They had formed groups and travelled by camel across the desert zones in the traditional way. Arms had been smuggled out of the Supply depots, and obsolete trucks, abandoned in the desert after the great battles of 1942/43, had been cannibalised and used again in civilian guise to transport the goods across the Suez Canal and thence to Gaza.

Our soldiers had fallen foul of such a group and, knowing nothing of these organisations, abandoned their trucks thinking that they had been surrounded by an unknown enemy. The poor ignorant soldiers got 28 days (guali-guali as they called army 'Jankers') detention and I, as the officer, was reprimanded because I had issued too much live ammunition to my men without instructions from higher authority!

Unfortunately for me, the man we wounded reported back to his leader who happened to be influential in Egyptian political circles and he complained to the Ministry of the Interior that an Egyptian national had been attacked by the British Army. Thus, G.H.Q. had been embarrassed and I had to be disciplined! The British Army had pointed out, however, that 'persons unknown' had stolen the equipment of an allied nation and that we should claim compensation if any further action was taken against the British officer and soldiers in question!

CHAPTER EIGHT

We turn back again

This involuntary spurt of active service had brought us to the notice of G.H.Q. and our company was ordered to proceed to the Central Supply Depot for guard duty, and our mode of life changed once again.

Tel-el-Kebir, set between the large town of Zagazig in the Nile Delta and Ismailia at the head of the Sweetwater Canal where it enters Lake Timsah, was the site of a battle between the British and the forces of the Khedive in the 1880's.

Now, in 1946, we were battling again, for marauding parties of vagabonds, some on camels, started a persistent campaign to rob this vast British Army supply depot, sited just above the canal bank. We were encamped within the perimeter, and our task was to prevent intruders penetrating the wire or infiltrating the depot via trucks and army vehicles from other parts of the Command. Although the African soldiers were soon at patrol work and were accurate shots, their English was not good enough for them to be able to take turns at the gates where it was necessary to inspect the papers of all coming through. Thus, it fell to the British N.C.O.s and the junior officers to carry out these duties.

There were just four lieutenants, four British sergeants and Barny, our Captain, to cover the 24 hours, including day duty, on the gates and so we soon got tired and ratty. We had been joined by a very pleasant Czechoslovakian lieutenant named Stanislav, and after he had been alerted three times one night by weird noises and scuffling just outside the wire, he decided the time had come to investigate. There was great excitement when he carried a loaded Bren gun outside the gates and, having received no satisfactory response to his challenge, fired the whole magazine from his hip, spraying bullets in all directions. The sounds stopped abruptly and no more was heard that night. After that we were all on the qui vive and orders were given to load rifles while on patrol after dark. One night, all hell was let loose and, being on duty, I buckled on my revolver belt and dashed to the wire. My men were firing at some dark object scurrying away into the gloom. I inspected the wire and found evidence that the would-be invaders had wire cutters with them. We heard later that a gang from Zagazig had very nearly succeeded in penetrating our defences - seemed rather unnecessary since many items of clothing and kitchenware vanished every day from the Q.M. stores - definitely an inside job! Most men can be bought, but not often in the unusual way I now recount. Having finished our tour of duty, the unit was moved out into the Western Desert near El Alamein to guard German prisoners of war who, by this time, were allowed to organise their own administration prior to repatriation.

I spent several eerie starlit nights on duty listening to their beautiful singing of traditional songs before I was ordered to take a company of African soldiers on detachment to guard an ordnance depot some way to the East and about 30 miles from Mex, the industrial suburb of Alexandria, well-known for its tanning works. For me this was a very lonely job. I was the only Englishman and my daily contact with H.Q. was by radio. No-one came to see me and I was continually on duty. A supply truck dumped our rations at the guard post gate twice a week. I resented this treatment very much, not only for myself but also for the soldiers who were virtually confined to the camp in their rest periods since there was nowhere to go and we had no transport.

The depot was stacked to the fence with brand new tanks and trucks from the U.S.A., which we understood had been destined for use by the Turks under the UNRRA agreement, but were never required. They were very valuable as general replacements, however, and I was expected to keep my men vigilant 24 hours a day against the accustomed marauding bands of robbers.

I had insisted that the perimeter wire should be checked before I took over this job, and the big gates at the only entrance were always lit after dark, with a guard post at each side. I organised a command post in my large tent which was set three feet down in the desert gravel; quite comfortable really especially in this Mediterranean climate near to the sea. Unfortunately, an escarpment carrying the main coast road masked us from any view of the water which was about three miles away, too far to organise bathing parties for the men. A pity, since this would have reduced their boredom somewhat.

One evening I was in my tent, mending a puncture in the tyre of one of the three push bicycles which had been sent up with the rations, and quietly listening to Vera Lynn on the Forces radio frequency, when the hurricane lamp blew out. I called to Fred Katsina, my batman, for a replacement but there was no response. I noticed that the whole camp was in darkness but was aware of scuffing noises in the tents around me. I became suspicious and opened the tent flap to be met by one of the African sergeants carrying an unlit hurricane lamp.

"What are you doing?" I said, "Light that lamp immediately."

"Sorry, Sah, I have dropped the matches."

"Well, pick them up quickly and let's have some light."

When we eventually got some light I noticed men moving about in all directions.

"What's going on, Sergeant? Why are the men so

restless?"

The sergeant didn't answer, appeared to trip, dropped the lamp and it went out. Darkness again - Oh, my God, what is going on, I thought.

"Get up, man" I said "and relight that lamp."

Finally, we got some light and I pushed past the stammering sergeant and made my way to the guardroom at the gate. I found no guard on duty and the arc lights extinguished. The gates were open! Lord, what had happened?

"Go, find the sergeant-major and tell him to report to me immediately" I shouted, "then round up the guard, shut the gates and put the gate lights on."

A lot more scuffling and then an old covered truck shot out through the gates. I dashed towards the gates and saw a man in a dirty white robe run from the guard post. Obviously not one of us, I thought, and gave chase. I managed to grab his robe and prevented him from leaving the compound. He struggled, but by this time the sergeant-major had arrived to help and between us we dragged the Arab back into the guard post. He was quite young and his eyes glinted in the half light filtering through the windows from the gate. We pushed him into a chair and demanded an explanation. Of course, he remained mute and we got nothing out of him - no doubt he could understand English but he wasn't going to admit it.

"Get on the 'phone to the local Caracol (Police station) and request that a police escort should come out to question him. I will contact our H.Q. by radio and tell them that we have trouble here. After that, call all the sergeants together and tell them to account for all their men and the stores."

"Yes, sah, I go."

An incredible story then unfolded. Some English-speaking Egyptians from Mex, knowing about our men's lack of entertainment, had suggested that they could introduce women to them at their camp in exchange for removing their guards for a couple of hours one evening so that these Egyptians could take payment, not in money but in moveable parts from the tanks and trucks in the compound! Our Africans were delighted, for they realised that we were only guarding surplus war stores and that the war was over. They were not allowed home for their own women so why not accept this generous offer? They would have to keep the officer and their N.C.O.s occupied while they had their fun and so they had planned to 'work shifts', as it were. One shift was to cause minor trouble around the camp to keep the sergeants busy, while Fred Katsina was to keep me happy with my bicycle tyre and the radio to dampen any sounds. I never found out what ruse they employed to keep the attention of the sergeant-major! Everything went to plan until the hurricane lamp in my tent went out!

We lost many speedos and clocks from the vehicles for the Egyptian police couldn't, or didn't, get the Arab in the dirty white robe to talk. He, apparently, had been left to cover the retreat of the women and the loot for we found a motorcycle hidden just outside our gates.

The soldiers faced a Court of Inquiry and our Major sentenced their leaders to 28 days' detention, and the rest were 'confined to barracks' for the same time. This was a farce since it was *because* the men had nowhere to go for entertainment outside the camp, that they had succumbed to being 'bought' through the enticement of human flesh!

The Major was pretty uncomplimentary to me, but since I complained very forcibly about lack of reliefs for a period of three months, he relented and I was posted to the pleasant U.N.R.R.A. camp for Jugoslav refugees at Tolombat on Abu Qir Bay, so famous for the Naval battle with the French during the Napoleonic wars. My platoon of African soldiers were there to 'guard' these poor refugees who had been loyal to General Mihailovich and had escaped from the agents of Tito when he gained power, with British help, in their country.

Actually, it was I who had to protect the pretty refugee girls from the advances of *our* soldiers. One of the girls, Svetlana, was detailed to look after me and although we had language difficulties, I rather enjoyed these attentions. We used to walk on the sea wall along the bay and gaze out towards our own homelands across the placid waters which had seen so much action in the 19th and 20th centuries. I often wonder what happened to this attractive girl who had been banished from her own country because she just happened to be on the wrong side politically. She was far too young to have understood the difference between Fascists and Communists!

CHAPTER NINE

Sand, Flies and Bandits

You will be posted to Cairo to carry out garrison duties and guard the railway marshalling yards, we were told.

At last we should be visiting the big city with its French, British and Moslem influences. Unfortunately, we discovered that we were to make a tented camp just across the boundary wire from Heliopolis, now the international airport for Cairo. Our convoy of trucks had to pass through the tree-lined avenues of the very fashionable modern suburb of Heliopolis to reach our destination.

What a contrast for us when we arrived. A piece of scrubland, formerly junkyard, had to be cleared before we could erect our tents. It was very hot and dry. Flies infested everything and within the week we all had tummy bugs and the M.O. had to be called in to treat not only the Whites but the African soldiers as well. Their jungle at home was full of wild life but at least they had learned to cope with it. Now they had been dumped, almost as cattle, in sight of a beautiful residential town with every modern hygienic device, but not even running water for them. All we could do was to give them extra rations and promise improvements later on. The officers were told that they could drive into the famous Gezira Club in Cairo one afternoon in the week or, of course, visit the city itself. The world-famous Club was technically on an island off the banks of the Nile and generations of British had built a horse-racing track, a golf course, tennis and squash courts and a glorious swimming pool frequented by the most beautiful girls, we swore, in the whole of the Middle East. We arrived feeling under-dressed and dirty from our rubbish dump, however, and we all needed a shower or bath before emerging on to the pool side. Most of the girls spoke French or Arabic, and this put us at a disadvantage. Barny, our Captain, could cope with the French, and got away to a good start. Not to be deterred, we lieutenants wallowed in the water waiting for our victims. My swimming was very basic but I was good at the back stroke. Half the time I didn't know where I was going and it wasn't long before I bumped into something beautifully soft. I turned to apologise and was confronted by Sue who swore at me like a trooper but in English! She happened to be an Army nurse stationed in Cairo and so my lonely days were over. I told her of our plight out on the rubbish dump and she was sympathetic.

"Absolutely disgraceful" she said, "no British Army unit would be stationed in such a spot in peacetime."

"Ah, but we are technically Africans while we are attached to W.A. units" I told her.

"Well, at least you could get a taxi to bring you in from Heliopolis" Sue said.

"If I can get away, would you show me around the city?"

"Love to," she said, "and that's if you take me to dinner afterwards."

"O.K., it's a date - I'll find a way of getting time off - where's the Nurses' Home?"

"Oh, that's easy, for it is between your camp and the centre of the city."

I managed to get away by 1700 hours one evening not long after, and soon we were walking hand in hand through the shopping streets of the metropolis. There were street vendors and newspaper stands everywhere, while near to the Nile bridges, sheep and goats were incongruously being driven into the markets from the outlying native suburbs.

The bridges reminded me of London's own river

crossings and when we finally went for dinner at Mena we crossed over the Bulacq bridge which connected with the long road to the Pyramids. The bridges are dominated by the imposing stone-built barracks and the famous museum buildings and we were to see student riots in this and the Central Station area before we were to move on to our next posting.

To entertain a girl in the pantiled courtyard of the Mena House restaurant is something to be remembered. The decor was opulent in the Franco-Arabesque style and had changed little since the 1920's. Vividly coloured drapes hung from the stone cornices, the semi-eliptic ceilings were painted with scenes from Egyptian antiquity and were supported by domed pillars much as in the temples at Luxor. We ordered kebabs and we drank Arak before our wine. Our hands met under the table as we marvelled at our luck to be in such a place with moonlight softly bathing the courtyard, still warm from the hot sun of the day. The sky was of blue velvet and my own miserable tent was a thousand miles away. I must have conveyed some of this feeling to Sue, for she sighed and told me about her life as a nurse and the discipline surrounding a military hospital in a foreign land. She was, of course, used to nursing discipline for she had trained in a London Hospital during the blitz before coming out to Egypt and had seen the most horrible consequences of the bombing. We were both civilians in uniform awaiting peace, which we assumed had now arrived. We were kidding ourselves that night, for 1946 was to bring the Palestine issue to a head and I began to understand why we had been attacked both at Tel-el-Kebir and in the Canal Zone by dissenting Egyptians who were tiring of a corrupt Royal regime and continued occupation by their wartime allies.

Tonight we were tourists and lovers, however, and I revelled in the warmth and closeness of the attractive girl by my side.

"Have you ever seen the Pyramids by moonlight?" I heard myself saying.

"No" she chuckled and I realised just how corny this remark had been. "But there's always a first time."

"Come on - let's take a taxi and go home via the Sphinx."

We did take in the silhouette of that strange creature, but we were really much too busy kissing and comforting one another to notice any more. Later, in daylight, we did spend a leave day at that most famous tourist rendezvous but neither of us rode a camel! I wanted to see much more of Sue.

Ah! Back to work and the rather daunting job of marshalling a convoy of lorries through the Railway Station Square, a meeting place for political activists from the Universities and from the Moslem Brotherhood; and on beside the station itself, to Fars Marshalling yard via narrow streets with overhanging balconies from which we were showered with foul water and worse, through a seething native market to the railyard where our African troops guarded vital army stores in transit from the ports of Alexandria and Port Said to the big depots such as Tel-el-Kebir.

We had been told that the Cairo students were becoming very restive and that they planned demonstrations against the British Army occupation, and the Western way of life in general. We suspected the Brotherhood who wished to return Egypt to the strict Moslem regime of the past. They had noted the first landings of Jewish refugees from Europe in the Holy Land and didn't believe that the British would keep them out of the territory around Jaffa as they had promised. I learned these facts from one of the students swimming with us at the Gezira Club pool and began to understand the complex nature of the Middle East problem as we now know it. Although the countries around the Eastern Mediterranean were vastly different, they were all Arabs and as such were deeply suspicious of the Jews.

While the students in those days were mostly well-to-do, the Fellahin of the Nile Delta lands were very poor and almost totally ignored by the rather mediaeval court of King Farouk. They showed their resentment by tipping chamber pots on our heads as we passed. Mind you, in my case, it only happened the first time we visited the yards. After that we protected the observation panels and side windows of the trucks in an appropriate manner!

I spent my day thinking of Sue and anticipating the pleasure of her company. We visited the Muski market and later we ate in a small Arab restaurant in central Cairo. After an excellent meal she consented to come with me to one of the many belly dancing exhibitions in the Night Clubs open to British troops. We had to be careful to keep within bounds, for we had heard of kidnappings and our own military police did not tolerate wayward troops who over-indulged themselves in the wicked city. British officers were more at home in Groppi's restaurant or at Shepherd's Hotel.

This pleasant existence did not last for many weeks, however, and soon we were told that we must go back to the Western Desert. While in Cairo I had heard that the Royal Corps of Signals officers were in short supply since general demobilisation had started, so I obtained an interview with a colonel at G.H.Q. and applied for transfer back to my own corps. Imagine my delight, therefore, when I was told to report to Signal H.Q., Alexandria, to take up the post of Signal Master.

I felt rather guilty in leaving my batman, Fred Katsina, and my signals platoon to their fate in this way, but I explained to them that I would remain in the army for only six further months before I returned to my home and civilian life. I knew that the Africans would also return to their villages by the end of 1946 and so we had a merry farewell party with much beer and African dancing. I had taken the precaution of inviting the Colonel (who politely declined) and my fellow officers to this colourful gathering and I ended up in my tent with a very thick head indeed.

I 'phoned Sue when I arrived at my new post and promised to visit her as soon as I could, but due to circumstances which I shall record, I never saw her again.

CHAPTER TEN

Alexandrian Experience

How good to be back in comfortable quarters once again. Mustapha barracks had been occupied by the British Army for over half a century and was situated close to the shore-line and adjacent to one of the fashionable beaches of Alexandria. Again, French influence everywhere but the traditional Egyptian buildings were centuries old and made of stone, many with over-hanging wooden balconies. The squares in the centre of the city were classical and the streets leading to harbour showed the Roman influence with Pharos, the ancient lighthouse of biblical days dominating the harbour mole. This was Royal Navy territory and I, as the signalmaster, could be invited to 'bring the (telephone) cable aboard'.

Now, I am not a good drinker and the first time I visited the Navy, I reeled off one of H.M. Destroyers very sick indeed! I preferred whisky to pink gin.

My own unit was responsible for all wireless and telegraphic services in the Alexandria district, down half-way to Cairo on the desert road and west to Mersa Matruh towards the Libyan border. We had radio communication with G.H.Q. Cairo, and later, a radio teleprinter link with America via Morocco and the Azores. I was no longer responsible for the defence of our communication systems - this was in the hands of an armoured car troop and there was a G.P.O. technical officer looking after the complicated terminal equipment at our sister barracks of Kom-el-Dik.

Social life was once more available to me and we had an attractive female Egyptian pay clerk named Penny who eventually introduced me to her friend who was a lovely Greek girl named Janni. I fell for her in a big way and promptly forgot Sue. I was able to meet her in the English tea house situated in a commanding position overlooking the crescent-shaped bathing beach. Fancy eating toasted tea cakes with a Greek girl in Egypt! It costs hundreds of pounds to visit such a resort today. It did occur to me that Janni had been asked to question me about my job in the Signals Office, and the movement order messages which we were sending more and more frequently now that demobilisation was in full flood. The Greeks in Alexandria ran much of the business in the city and they were very active in the cotton trade. Janni was exceedingly cross with Mr. Churchill for his treatment of the Greeks, and her family were obviously worried about their future if the British left Egypt. I invited her to join our idyllic bathing parties on the beach always attended by two Safragi waiters from the Sudan who had looked after the regular army officers for most of their working lives. The waiters erected a colourful rectangular tent on free afternoons and provided tea and goodies for the officers and their friends. This set-up reminded us of the Crusades and King Richard's court in the Holy Land.

The ladies, of course, wore smart one-piece bathing costumes at that time, but Janni and Penny looked to us every bit as glamorous as Queen Berengaria and her lady in waiting.

The beach below the barracks followed the curve of the bay and there was a single rock some twenty yards from the shore. With little tide and generally a warm calm sea, we chased each other backwards and forwards to this lump of volcanic matter for hours on end to drop exhausted on the sand for our tea.

It was the end of the Summer and the late afternoons were getting cold for Egypt, a mere 65°F, so we usually retreated to the bathing huts and hoped for a bit of a snog before returning to barracks.

The Officers' Mess was organised by these same Safragis with some attention to detail. They ensured that we passed the port correctly after our evening meal and then made delicious coffee!

By the Autumn of 1946 we were checking on our army release numbers and I noted that I could be out by Christmas. It was October, and we were told by G.H.Q. Cairo that we had been chosen to route a message from the battlefields of El Alamein to the first Alamein Reunion to be held in the Albert Hall, London. We knew that Monty was behind this move since he had been recently appointed Chief of the Imperial General Staff. Elaborate precautions were taken, therefore, to record the message and send it to London in advance and routed in three different ways. Everything went to plan and we celebrated in the Mess that night by inviting our lady friends. Highly irregular, but what did we care at this stage of the proceedings!

A sumptuous buffet was arranged, and Penny promised to bring Janni along. I knew that she had many boy friends, both Greek and English, and so I was flattered when she arrived looking lovely in a black dress - typically Greek, I thought. Although she flirted with the other officers, she seemed to like dancing with me and I decided that I must get her away from the mob. She told me about her family and the business they were in and I understood her distrust of the British authorities.

"Perhaps I could find some civilian clothes" I heard myself saying, "then I could take you to one of the restaurants in town."

"Good idea," she said "and then I can introduce you to

some of my friends."

At this juncture I received a signal to tell me that I had been promoted to Captain at last, and that from the 1st of November I should be in charge of the unit due to the demob of my immediate superior. What a thrill, since Janni was always telling me of her Guards Officer friends who had claimed that one of their lieutenants was equal to a Captain in any other army unit.

In my exalted position I could take the Signals jeep into town without prior permission, but where would I park it? So, I arranged for the regular driver to take me into the city 'on business' and then pick me up late in the evening. The driver didn't like this latter suggestion but the offer of an extra afternoon off did the trick and I duly called at Janni's house. To my surprise I was asked in and for a moment saw her mother and father who nodded politely. Her mother was slim and had glasses. She also wore the regulation black dress which I found to be a trifle odd for sophisticated Alexandria with its vivid silks displayed in almost every shop. I came to the conclusion that tradition dies very hard in nearly all parts of the world.

"We are going to a club where you will hear our traditional music" Janni told me. I was impressed for I had not visited Greece but I was interested in their dancing with the males leading with hands clasped. I drank their Rakki and became most talkative. "Time to go home" I was told, and Janni steered me towards the doors.

"Let's take a taxi up to the head of the Bay" I suggested.

"All right, so long as we are home by midnight" she said. I kissed her ear for the first time and she tasted delicious.

"Stop that" she said, but cuddled into me. The night was all warm velvet and I wished it could go on for ever.

"Let's do this again - can we?"

"Yes" she said quietly, "but first I have been asked to a

party at the villa of a member of the Italian royal family and need a partner - will you come with me?"

"Of course I will, but what about uniform?"

"No - not in uniform" she said quickly and I got the drift. She liked me for myself and not for my uniform. This made me feel very good indeed.

A signals jeep would not have done for this occasion and so I ordered a limousine from the most reputable taxi company in Alexandria and hired a white tuxedo from the little 24 hour tailor who was the Egyptian alternative to Moss Bros.

I wondered what it would be like to visit the home of royalty even if they had been deposed because of their compliance with the unfortunate activities of the dictator Mussolini. Janni will know the drill, I assured myself. She seemed so self-confident and full of life, and when I called for her, she looked stunning in a long white dress with slim crossover straps revealing her pretty shoulders and firm white breasts. I swallowed hard and hoped that she had not noticed my nervousness. "Hello David" she whispered and my heart turned over several times before I took her hand and guided her into the back seat of the car. She cuddled up and told me to follow her moves when we were introduced to her friends, the princesses.

"They're just like the rest of us now they live in Egypt" she told me.

The villa was situated on high ground overlooking another bay to the west of our beach crescent. The architecture was of French influence and impressive steps led up to an ornate double front door which now stood open with light and merry sound emanating from it. We were met by a Safragi major domo dressed in white with a brilliant red sash around his shoulders and waist. He shepherded us to our hostesses who looked very elegant but turned out to be most friendly.

"Chao, Janni, who is your boy friend?"

"He is an Englishman stationed in Egypt" she explained.

"Do find yourselves some drinks and later on we shall have a band for dancing."

With this, the ladies moved off to greet more new arrivals.

"Let's see if we can find Penny and her boy friend from the Provo's office" said Janni. We glided through the marble hall to the main salon which faced the Mediterranean, and the sliding windows were open to the terrace and a beautiful rose garden surrounded by cyprus trees. November in Alexandria is a month of temperate weather and clear nights, and in later years I wondered why I was so anxious at this time to return home to civilian life. However, at this moment I only had eyes for Janni who simply sparkled. I managed to get the first dance with her but then she received offers from the many handsome males present. There were Frenchmen, Greeks, some Italians, of course Egyptians and, worst of all, British Guards officers. The latter impressed Janni and she had already informed me that the Guards had told her their lieutenants were equal to our captains! To my consternation, the Guards had turned up in uniform and there were quite a few members of the aristocracy amongst them. One particular lieutenant was most attentive and I had to use all my ingenuity to get the last dance with Janni. I did complain to her but she told me to be a good boy and not be jealous. After all, I had been asked as her escort not her keeper. This blunted my ardour somewhat and I took her straight home, but with the promise that she would meet me at the English Teahouse the next afternoon when I came off duty.

I waited with some impatience for teatime to come and arrived early in my anxiety. The waiters had only just come on duty for I was the first customer and all the tables had not yet been set. The whole place reeked of the Colonial past and I had the feeling that I was witnessing the end of an era. Never mind, a lovely girl was to arrive at any minute and I realised that I must have her for myself.

Who were these damned Guards Officers, anyway? I realised that I had been sitting at the table for about half an hour now and no Janni! The waiter came across and asked me if I wished to order tea. I said that I would wait for my guest; he grinned and moved away. After an hour, I thought I had better order for one and it dawned on me that I had been stood up. Janni could have 'phoned the Teahouse but no word came. There had better be a good explanation, I muttered to myself, and I realised that I was becoming most possessive. Did this mean that I was truly falling in love with a foreign girl? Perhaps she was testing me to see whether I had serious intentions towards her.

I returned to the barracks with a heavy heart and full of confused feelings. Should I confide in Penny and ask her to call at Janni's house to discover what had happened? Maybe there was a simple explanation - or had she dated one of those Guards Officers? They did have a most attractive mess in one of the city hotels and they could give the girls a marvellous time.

Penny could not, or would not, pass me any news of Janni - I did find out that she had been seen with one of the Guards Officers, however, but that her parents had decided to return to Greece and that she was expected to find a Greek husband when she got to Athens. I was still infatuated with Janni, and managed to pass a message inviting her to our Christmas party in the old barracks mess. She couldn't resist this invitation and agreed to come along with Penny.

Some of the other girls had volunteered to cook omelettes at the party, much to the disapproval of the

Safragi waiters, and to my surprise Janni took my hand and led me into the kitchens so that she could join them. She put on an apron and motioned me to pass her the eggs.

As usual, drink was flowing in great quantities and most of us had become very merry. Janni had just produced my omelette when, by general approval, it was agreed that we should take the 'cooks' to our own quarters for the meal with, of course, a fresh bottle of wine each. First, I thought that Janni wouldn't come with me, but suddenly she made up her mind and we left the mess. "My room isn't much, I'm afraid" I heard myself say, "but you sit in the chair and I'll sit on the bed."

"That's not very friendly - I'll come and sit with you - here's a fork, eat your omelette."

We fell into pleasant drunken silence while we were eating and when we had finished, she turned to me and looked directly into my eyes.

"I owe you an apology, sweetie" she said. "I wanted to meet you at the Tea House that afternoon, but my father forbade me because he thought that you didn't have honourable intentions towards me. I told him not to interfere and let me run my own life, but we are Catholics and Greek families are very strict about relationships outside marriage. You might have heard that our family is returning to Greece now peace has come; you British will go home and leave Egypt to some new regime. Oh! everything is so uncertain for me - I don't know what to do" she said.

"I thought you had taken up with a Guards Officer - won't he marry you?"

"That's a rotten thing to say, David."

She was now sobbing and I pulled her to me and stammered that I hadn't meant to be bitchy.

"You've never mentioned love to me anyway, so why should I carry on with you - the Guards are fun, that's all."

"Oh, Janni - I do love you and I've been bitterly unhappy not seeing you."

"So have I, darling - but I know that you will be going home soon and I can't afford to love you."

"That's not right - no doubt we can work something out - hush now, darling and kiss me."

She flung herself into my arms and held me tight. We snatched love while we could and my bed experienced emotions quite equal to anything during the previous half century of its use. I'm afraid we saw no more of the other party guests that night.

I had a touch of guilty conscience when I received a letter from Marjorie at this point in my relationship with Janni. I had heard nothing from her for months and my new preoccupation had put her to the back of my mind. She explained why she had not written before and asked me to note her new address. It was in the British zone of occupied Germany and she was working as a medical secretary in a military hospital. She sounded most enthusiastic about her new job and she had met interesting people including some of my army colleagues of pre-invasion days who had campaigned from the Normandy beachheads all the way to Germany with one of the Signals units I should have joined. The stores which my men had so stoutly 'willed' onto that ship in London Docks had been put to good use, it seemed. She wondered when I would be returning to U.K. and how I was getting on.

This letter made me feel less worried since Marjorie was obviously enjoying her life once again and had obviously buried her sorrows in the past. We had been very close for that short time before I left England and I did feel that I had an obligation to her and she *was* an attractive English girl after all. I realised that I should now be thinking of what I would do with my life when I eventually returned home. I had been offered a job with prospects if I could persuade the boss that I was capable of settling down, and there was no reason why I should not marry. Janny was 100% woman and I was desperately attracted to her but she was a sun-worshipping girl from Greece and I had to admit that I couldn't see her presiding over a woman's coffee party in suburban Surrey!

CHAPTER ELEVEN
The Final Turn

Christmas euphoria was quickly shattered by a tragic incident. I was resting, half-asleep in my room after duty when there was a loud bang!

It was early evening and most of my men were off duty. They were accustomed to spend many hours in the cosmopolitan bars which surrounded the old Barracks and they had made many friends but also a lot of enemies.

I reached for my revolver belt and went down into the quadrangle to investigate. The acrid smell of cordite stung my nostrils and I saw that two men were kneeling beside a third.

"The bastards have got Higgins, Sir," said one of my corporals.

"What's happened - is he still alive?"

"No, Sir, they must have lobbed a grenade over the wall quite near to him for there are bits of shrapnel embedded in his uniform and look at his bloodied face."

"My God, what a thing to do at a time of goodwill - better get a stretcher and take him to the medical room, Corporal - I will contact the Military Police to make the necessary enquiries but I doubt whether they will catch the swine who did this. Either a political agitator or riff-raff from one of the bars, no doubt. Oh, and arrange for the main gate to be closed until further notice. We don't want the troops going out to take the law into their own hands, do we?"

"No sir, I'll take the necessary action straight away but I doubt if the boys will take this lying down."

The corporal moved off at the double.

There was a near riot when the rest of my Squadron

heard the news from the signalmen who had witnessed this horrible event and I had to do some persuasive talking to restrain them from leaving the barracks with the avowed intent of ransacking all the cafés in the vicinity!

Of course, there was an enquiry but the bomber was never found and Signalman Higgins didn't get *his* demob. This had been only one of the hundreds of such bombing incidents to be recorded over the next few years in a politically unsettled world of so-called peacetime!

On New Year's Day 1947, I learned why my army release had not materialised. The Alexandrian Sector of the Western Desert was to be evacuated within a few weeks.

A Hirings and Disposals Officer joined our Mess and I spent hours going through schedules of arms and equipment with him. He was an amusing fellow whose rich Spanish father had sent him to an English public school which he had left at the outbreak of war to return to his Lebanese mother and the rest of his family in Egypt.

We had inherited over 200 vehicles surplus to our establishment due to the continued reduction of troops since the war had moved on into Italy and beyond. Some of these vehicles were comic. The chassis of one of them had been reversed to form a cradle for telegraph pole handling, with a replacement engine taken from a mobile bath unit!

"There are only 30 drivers in my unit so what happens to the unwanted hardware?" I asked.

"Oh! We can flog this lot quite easily to the locals - better than having them nicked," grinned my new friend "Come back to my house and meet the family. We can talk again in more pleasant circumstances, I think."

By mid-January 1947 all was prepared for our handover to the Egyptian Army but first it was the turn of the Navy to receive the Egyptian Naval Commandant who sailed into Alexandria Harbour on a ship whose crew had the greatest difficulty in raising their own flag. In fact a couple of British tars had to help them! Two days later it was my turn to do the honours, and an Egyptian army Major swept into our barracks driving an old command vehicle which possibly had seen service in the Battle of Alamein.

During the autumn of 1946, the remaining British officers had been summoned to a secret meeting in Cairo, and were ordered to retain duplicates of all unit diagrams and plans in case they were to be needed in later years.

I was now told to proceed to Port Said in civvy clothes with our own unit's line diagrams and await a ship home. As I left, I learned that yet another robber gang had stolen tons of valuable metal from the now unguarded co-axial telephone cable stretching from Alexandria to Mersa Matruh which the Egyptian State Telephone Company had purchased for a great deal of money only the night before!

It was wonderful to be free of responsibility for a few days and I spent some fascinating hours sitting on the balcony of the Officers' transit hotel watching those same Feluccas quietly plying their trade - come war, come peace - as they had done for the last four thousand years.

As I watched the warm sun setting over the Plage d'Enfants beach at Port Fuad on the last evening before embarkation, I wondered what life had in store for me when I arrived in England.

I woke up to find that a ship had berthed and that there was a signal to tell me that I should report on board at 10.30 hours.

Many Service families from India were on board and since the British Raj were beginning to hand over their responsibilities to the Indians, some of the British other ranks were travelling home, after long service, with Indian wives and children. I spent many hours talking to them and learned of their apprehensions - what would England be like after the war? Did it rain all the time?

"No," I told them, "but I have heard that prolonged heavy snow has made communications very difficult. You'll have to wrap up very warm when you land."

We saw no more sun after turning north at Cape St. Vincent and when we reached Liverpool on a darkening February afternoon, during a power cut, the ship ground against an icy quay which was covered with snow. What a welcome, we all thought. At this moment I heard a shout of anguish coming from the seaward side of the ship.

"Man overboard! Man overboard!" exclaimed a hoarse voice. Some of us dashed over to see what could be done. One of the seamen had thrown a yellow life-buoy out to a struggling figure who was flailing the water with frenzied arms. A brown head with tousled black hair disappeared beneath the white-grey water and was finally lost to us. Having recognised his voice I realised that the victim was the very wife of the English sergeant to whom I had been so recently talking. The sight of our cold, bleak country must have been just too much for her to accept and perhaps in a moment of panic she had taken this impulsive action. Her confused children clung to their father in his grief and we left them huddled together but, at least, with sympathetic Welfare workers by their side.

After we had disembarked and were standing shivering on the quay waiting to hear whether our train could negotiate the Pennines to reach the de-mob centre in this horrible weather, I thought again about my overpowering wish to get home from the sunshine of Egypt. Perhaps it had been the fear of losing the chance of release from the Forces after all this time, but in my heart of hearts I knew that it was more the homing instinct and the thought of seeing my family again, and Marjorie.